BECOMING JOANNE

2

Deepening his sissy feminization

Lady Alexa

Also by Lady Alexa

Becoming Joanne
Becoming Joanne 1
Becoming Joanne 2
Becoming Joanne 3

Femboy Love
Femboy Love

Feminized and Pretty
Feminized and Pretty 1
Feminized and Pretty 2
Feminized and Pretty 3
Feminized and Pretty 4

Lockdown Feminization
Lockdown Feminization 3
Lockdown Feminization 1

Sissy femboy transgender husband
Sissy Husband 2
Sissy Husband 3
Sissy Husband 1
Sissy Husband 4

Sissy Princess
Sissy Princess 2
Sissy Princess 1

Stepmother's Sissy
Stepmother's Sissy
Stepmother's Sissy 2
Stepmother's Sissy 3

Standalone
Maid To Serve
A Very Dominant Woman
Feminized By My Wife
Female Transformation
Samantha's Law
An Accidental Girl
The Mother-In-Law Dilemma

In book one of Becoming Joanne, we met Joseph who had been a very bad husband. His wife Julie asked her best friend, the high-powered lawyer Melissa, to teach Joseph a lesson. Melissa put him to work in her office as an admin. assistant and gradually forces him into female clothing and renames him, Joanne.

In book two, Melissa takes Joseph/Joanne into her own home to increase his humiliation and his transformation into a submissive girl; Joanne. She employs a personal beautician and a strict female ex-army officer to guide him into the next stage of becoming Joanne.

Prologue

My name is Joanne. I'm a 45-year-old housewife and this is part 2 of my unusual story in the Becoming Joanne series.

I wasn't always a pretty housewife, I used to be a man called Joseph. I was a rather difficult husband, to put it mildly, and I finally pushed my long-suffering wife Julie too far. I drank too much, screwed around with young girls and relied on her to keep me financially. Book 1 told the story of how Julie asked her friend Melissa for help. Melissa: The very name still makes me shudder.

Melissa's 'great idea' was to employ me at her own company which was a legal office in which she was the CEO and lead lawyer. I was totally dependent on Julie financially so I had to do what Melissa told me. If not, Julie would throw me out of the marital home and out on the street. I'd have nothing.

Melissa put me to work as the administrative assistant. She became uncomfortable with me being the only male there so she tricked me into wearing female clothing. First in the office and then at my home after she destroyed all my male clothing. I was forced to wear skirts and dresses all the time.

Melissa and Julie had always told me that once I'd learnt my lesson, they would allow me to go back to being a proper male. I tried so hard to behave and pretend that I was a reformed character. Melissa wasn't convinced and Book 2 relates what she called the next stage of my re-education and transformation.

My name is Joanne and I'm not sure I will ever be allowed to be Joseph again. Maybe I don't want to be any more.

1 Pierced

My erection strained and pointed to the ceiling like an accusing finger to my past behaviour. My short dress was up on my stomach and my panties were around my ankles

I laid on my back, flat down on a high clinical-style bed in the back room of a high-street beauty parlour. I cowered as Tia, the uncomfortably attractive young beautician, who would have been my type once upon a time, held an ear-piercing staple gun. She chatted with my wife Julie as the gun waved inches from the end of my erect penis.

Julie giggled as she swung my pink plastic cock cage on the end of an index finger. The grumbling sound of traffic on the high street filtered into the room from the front of the shop. Tia's eyes flitted down every few seconds to my erect penis and then to my neat triangle of pubic hair, the only air on my body below my head. A look of surprised elation was etched across her triangular face.

Tia looked serious for a moment. "I've put plenty of Prince Albert rings into men's..." She hesitated for a short moment. "Willies before." Her eyes wavered to me, Julie and Melissa. She sniggered. "But I've never done it to a man who was wearing a short yellow summer dress and pink women's shoes before."

Melissa advised me earlier that day that I was going for *beauty treatment*. Now I understood that she didn't mean a facial. The truth of the expedition faced me in the form of the device about to puncture my penis. It was numb after Tia had put a numbing cream over it. That was why I was erect even though she'd used gloves.

"Er, Tia," I said. "I don't want a Prince Albert ring."

Tia's large over-made-up blue eyes flicked to Melissa. "Ignore her, she's just nervous. Sissy's are cowards, they want to be sissies but shudder a little bit of discomfort."

I shifted my pleading to my wife, Julie. "I'm a reformed person, no more affairs, no more drunkenness. I'll work diligently," I promised, my voice cracking.

Julie folded her arms and tutted. "Too late for that Joanne," she said, "You had your chance and blew it."

A pulse throbbed in my temple. My erect penis towered in my eye-line. A fading symbol of my masculinity, denuded of pubic hair and respect. It was awaiting another step in its emasculation.

I wanted to flee this place but Melissa's glare pinned me back. It was enough to remind me of the consequences if I didn't do as she ordered.

Melissa stood upright and emotionless at the bottom of the bed, a fixed glare on her hard-set, yet oddly alluring face. Her features were large, her eyes like brown ripe almonds. Her arms were folded high and her face and lips were set tight. Her long red-brown tussled hair was thick, shiny and full of body. It fell over her eyes and bare shoulders. She wore a tight short red dress that hugged her voluminous breasts.

My fingers twitched, wanting to caress and fondle them and bury my face between those two mounds of sex and power. No chance. Ever.

A black frill around the hem of her dress was lined across her slim muscular legs. My erection ached for her. I didn't want to have such a strong desire for her, she was belligerent and aggressive towards me. The problem was that the worse she treated me, the more I wanted her. Why did she have to be so damn sexy?

"I don't want to pierce his penis until his erection has gone down. The skin is too tight and everything is..." She batted her eyes in what seemed like exasperation. "Swollen."

I shuddered, becoming more desperate. My throat was tight and dry.

Julie thought the whole event was highly amusing. I didn't know what had got into her, she used to be so gentle and pliant. That's what I used to like about her. She had changed and I blamed Melissa.

Melissa tapped her foot. "I'm sure it'll be fine." She looked at her watch. "I'm running out of time, Tia. Can't you get on with it?" Then her face softened. "I'm going to attach a little bell to the ring once you've put it in."

Julie laughed loud and I hoped she was joking, turning the screw of my humiliation.

The salon's back room had no air-conditioning and my skin was clammy in the summer heat. The room was small and there was only space for Tia and her client.

My balls lay flat and loose in the heat against the starched white paper cover like two spread-eagled plucked chicken legs waiting to be roasted. The smell of fresh paint from the newly decorated pastel green walls swirled in my nostrils with the perfumed scent from an air freshener. There was bile in my throat, whether that was the smell or the impending piercing was not clear. The idea of Tia piercing my tender penis head sent a cold chill over my hot skin.

Several jars of cream and cotton wool balls for pedicures and facials sat on the top of a chrome table to the side of my bed. I had thought these were the reason for the visit; now I knew otherwise. The piercing implement in the beautician's raised hand caught the glint of the fluorescent lighting. I shivered despite the oppressive heat, the thought of what she was soon to do was all too imminent.

Behind Tia and Julie, a white curtain separated us from the salon outside. Tia hadn't pulled it fully across and I could see two women having their nails done by attendants in white face masks with elastic straps around their ears. The attendants glanced at me from time to time with cold unblinking eyes. I rubbed the back of my neck to wipe away the sweat, my long straightened blonde hair stuck to my skin.

Beyond the attendants, the late morning July sunlight streamed in through the shop-front windows. I asked Tia to close the curtain properly. Melissa barked at me to shut up and to lose the erection, "We're all waiting, Joanne." There was dislike in her eyes.

I wanted to run as Melissa's glare intensified as I fidgeted in intense discomfort from the heat and the situation. If I didn't accept the piercing, I would lose my job with her and be evicted from my home. Or more accurately, the home owned by my wife Julie's parents. I'd be on the street, penniless with only women's clothes to wear. I was trapped. It was only two days ago that Melissa had led the destruction of all my male clothing and replaced them with an all-female wardrobe. I now had only skirts and dresses, panties and women's high-heeled shoes.

"Do her ears first then we'll come back to the Prince Albert ring." Melissa's face remained fixed, impassive. It was as if a man with an exposed erection in a summer dress about to have a penis ring inserted were an everyday occurrence

I sat up. "Ears, what do you mean ears?" Each new piece of information unwrapped her unwanted present to me, hitting me like tiny arrows flying into my head.

Tia moved over and clipped the staple gun on my left earlobe and pressed as I glared at Melissa. Click. I felt a sharp pain. I squealed an, "*Ow,*" and put my hand to my lobe; it met a new small circular metal ring. Tia leant across me as I touched the now tender lobe. Her small breasts brushed against my chest and, for a moment, excitement shot through my skin. It passed as quickly as it had arrived when another sharp pain hit my other lobe.

Tia moved back, her elbow brushed against my erection. "She looked embarrassed and mouth, "Sorry."

My hard penis swung lazily in the hot air. She looked down at it, her face flushed embarrassed. She shuffled away, eyes down.

I held both hands before my eyes. There were spots of blood on both fingertips. I had earrings. I had pierced ears! Things were escalating and I didn't know how to stop them. Julie's eyes widened and then she fell into another fit of giggles. Melissa looked at her watch again as her foot tapped out her impatience.

A hand on the curtain caught my eye. A young lady in a white top ducked her head into the crowded room and asked Tia for a face cream. She spotted my erection, red and primed like a missile about to take off. A trickle of pre-cum dribbled down the stem and to the back of my balls. Her eyes followed it for a few moments as her mouth dropped. She mumbled, "*Sorry,*" and shot out leaving the curtain even further open.

"I can't wait any more, I've got things to do. Pass me those rubber gloves." Melissa snatched the gloves from a nervous Tia, snapped them on and grabbed my erection. I squealed as she pulled at my erection. "I want that ring in her clitty now."

Melissa held my penis in both gloved hands. "Now. Tia. Do it."

Tia's hands moved in a blur as she clipped the piercing tool on and pressed. Cold metal hit my exposed penis head. A bolt of pain shot into my stomach despite the numbing cream. I screamed. She withdrew it and a gold ring sat through the end of my penis, through the end and out of the top.

Melissa let go and it slid back to expose my red bulbous penis head with a large golden ring attached. Despite that shock, I wanted to cum. That wasn't going to happen, Melissa had banned that. Melissa ripped off her surgical gloves and dropped them on the floor. She fished in her handbag and produced a small cat bell. She lifted it and, for the first time that morning, her closed lips turned up at the edges. She rang the tiny bell by the side of her head. *Tinkle tinkle.* She clipped it on the new ring and told me to stand up. She hadn't been joking about the bell. I was mortified to see this new symbol of my utter humiliation. A pet's bell?

Tia made an excuse. "My next customer is waiting." She left through the half-open curtain in haste.

I slid off the bed to the sound of a tinkle from the bell hanging from my hard penis. The hem of my dress fell over the top of my erection, framing it in yellow cotton. I fought back the anger at Melissa's latest trick. I had to calm down, I wasn't going to win any debate with her. I'd only make the situation even worse.

"Walk Joanne. Hold your dress up to your stomach." Melissa's hands folded again across her body.

I shuffled around the tiny room with my panties around my ankles. My straining erection was out firmly at right angles to my body, the ring with the hanging bell leading the way. Each shuffle produced a tinkle from the bell and a clack from my high heels.

Tinkle clack tinkle clack. I turned and shuffled back. *Tinkle clack tinkle clack*. Julie snorted through her nose and her giggles continued. She seemed drunk on my humiliation.

"Excellent." Melissa's calculating cool eyes followed my bouncing erection as I moved.

I pushed my hair away from my neck to get some air to it. My finger brushed against my new earring. I'd forgotten about that in my humiliation at the ring and the bell now attached to my penis.

Melissa stroked her chin and my stomach turned over in desire and worry at what she might be thinking. I let the front of my dress go and it fell over my erect penis. The loose cotton of the dress stood out over the erection, but at least I was covered. My panties hung around my ankles. I knew to wait for Melissa's instruction as to when I could pull them up.

"We need to get back, I have work to do," she announced after some thought. She marched out of the room. She stopped on the other side of the open curtain. She had forgotten something. Spinning around, she told me to step out of my panties. "Let some air get to the little puncture wound in your clitty."

I recoiled at the mention of a wound in my penis.

Julie followed her as she marched off towards the salon door. I waddled behind her, *tinkle clack, tinkle clack, tinkle clack*. Bell ring then heel click, bell ring, heel click. The two attendants and their customers' eyes followed me. I put my head down and headed for the door.

Melissa had also noticed the people staring at me. "They can see you're a sissy Joanne," she said too loudly for my comfort. "It's because you still walk like a man, even in those high heels."

A look of worry came to Julie's face. "Melissa, I know we're teaching him a lesson, but maybe we've gone too far in this humiliation making it so public?" Her voice rose.

I watched as my wife and Melissa squared up to each other. Julie always looked as if she was permanently cold with red cheeks and red nose against chalk-white skin. Her face was pinched and her body too slim and boyish. I had been attracted to her because she was pliable, timid and more than a little gullible. She thought the best of everyone which was useful for my regular sessions with the many young ladies I came into contact with. Until I pushed her too far and she enlisted Melissa to teach me a lesson by feminising and humiliating me. Hope filled my chest that she was calling time on the whole *feminise and humiliate Joseph* game. I was too dependent on her money and support.

"And just how has this gone too far, Julie?" Melissa's voice was low, a menace vibrated beneath the tone. "She." Melissa pointed her finger at me, almost touching my nose but looking straight at Julie. "Treated you like a fool for years, abusing your kindness and now we have her under control. At last. What's your problem with this? I think she needs to remain a sissy girl for a good while longer."

My stomach turned over in shock. I thought this feminisation thing was just a warning shot to show me things from a woman's perspective. I didn't like the sound of her statement, *'For a good while longer'*. I now hoped that Julie would take back control, but I knew in my heart that she was not strong enough to counter her best friend.

A friend she admired and respected deeply. If Melissa said something then that was the way things were, as far as Julie was concerned.

"I know, Melissa." Julie looked down, her pinched cheeks reddened to a beetroot shade. "He is my husband, so I thought…"

Melissa's face softened. "Julie, it's she and Joanne. She can't be your husband any more, she's your housewife now." Melissa put her fingers under Julie's chin and raised her head.

Everyone in the shop had stopped what they were doing and were watching Melissa and Julie; it was as if they were a part of some bizarre TV soap opera.

"Yes I'm sorry, Melissa, you're right."

For a moment, I'd had some hope that Julie would be tough. My hope was dashed. I should have known. I did know in my heart.

"But…," Julie said and her face reddened even more. Was she about to stand up to Melissa after all?

"I don't want her to suffer too much and, besides, she still looks like a man which could cause her and us a few problems in the street."

I could have hugged her, she was standing up for me after all. If only a little. A wave of love went to her and I felt a twang of guilt for the way I'd treated her over the years. I willed her to tell Melissa I could change back to male clothing.

Julie dug into her handbag and pulled out an oversized pair of female sunglasses. "Joanne could wear these as a disguise. They would hide her slightly masculine face." Without waiting she placed them on my face.

Melissa sighed through her nose in despair. "You're such a softy, Julie, that's why I love you." She then opened the shop door and marched out. Julie had won just a tiny victory for me but I remained feminised. Better than nothing was the best I could grasp from the situation.

Outside in the street, I kept my sunglasses-covered eyes focused on the pavement below my feet. I hadn't been spotted on the way into the shop as I had been dropped off at the shop door front. Julie parked the car afterwards. Now we had to walk for ten minutes to the car park.

The July heat beat on my thick straightened hair. The passing traffic masked the sound of the bell as it hit the underside of my erection in time with my steps. I had to be thankful for small mercies.

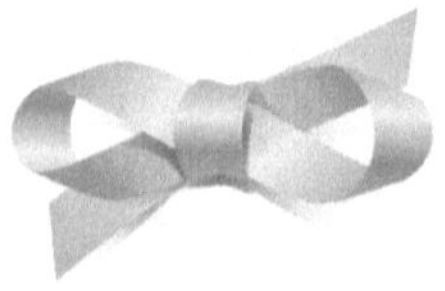

2 A Home Girl

I sat in the rear seat on the way home. It was no longer a home though, it was the house where I lived with Julie. It no longer felt like home in the way it had. What had I got myself into? I was kicking myself for allowing Melissa to control me and I couldn't see a way out of my current mess. She had feminised and humiliated me at her office, put me in girl's clothes and now made me have pierced ears and a pierced penis. And that little bell. I snorted in futile anger.

Melissa had orchestrated the destruction of my male clothes like a femdom conductor; I had only female clothes to wear.

A dull throb from down below reminded me of my recent piercing in that very tender area. I pulled my dress over it and put my knees apart in an unladylike way to avoid my penis touching my thighs. Every little bump made the bell ring. Julie was sitting in the front as Melissa drove and her shoulders and head moved up and down in fits of laughter as the bell tinkled. Melissa remained impassive.

We pulled into the driveway and I rushed to the front door. I wanted no one to see me this way. The neighbours would surely recognise me, even in the dress and heels. The little bell stopped tinkling as I waited by the door. This was worse than I imagined it could be when Melissa started on me. I wondered when it would stop and they decided that I'd learnt my lesson. Not for a while, Melissa had said. How long was a while?

Julie opened the door after a far too casual stroll to me. Once indoors, Melissa told me to sit in the kitchen and Julie would bathe my clitty in salt water to help it heal. I wasn't allowed to touch my penis. Another of Melissa's new rules. I was feeling the freedom of not wearing the dreaded chastity cage that Melissa had added to the rules. Julie and Melissa each had a key to my cage and they would unlock me only when they were around to keep an eye on me. I had to urinate with the door open, sitting down. Only if I was doing something else would I be allowed to shut the door. The cage stayed on t other times though.

Julie put a bowl of warm salty water on the kitchen table and bathed my sore penis head with cotton wool. I let myself enjoy this despite Melissa scowling at me with her legs apart and hands on her hips. She wasn't happy that I had an erection. She knew I was enjoying it. I took small things these days.

Every time Julie wiped the little bits of dried blood away, the bell tinkled. It was driving me crazy already. I looked through to the dining area that was open from the kitchen. Something was missing.

My guitar used to sit in the corner. It was no longer there. I know I hadn't played it for many years but I liked to see it and imagine I was a rock star. Then I noticed my pictures of old vinyl album covers had been replaced with black and white photos of beaches and stones. I sat up. The open kitchen shelves where I'd had my CDs and books on football now had ornaments of china teapots and little animals. Julie had erased my personality from our home and replaced it with bland femininity.

Melissa chose that moment to remind me I was not allowed to cum. I was desperate, I hadn't cum for some days which was unusual for me. In the past if Julie had been tired or that time, it mattered little as there was always a young chick somewhere who'd fall for my charms and chat.

Now I needed relief and I couldn't see how I would manage it. How had I got myself into this mess? I'd been too careless and I thought I was invincible. Now I'm forced to wear female clothing, a female hairstyle and made to have earrings. It was my fault, I knew that. I had pushed Julie too far in the end. I didn't realise she knew about all my affairs. How did she know? I had been so careful and I didn't think she was that bright. I had misjudged her and she'd turned the tables on me. I would have no chance of an affair now. Not dressed like this and especially with a chastity cage locked around my penis.

"Once you've learnt your lesson, girl, we'll let you go. Until that time, this is how things will be." Melissa watched Julie dabbing at my penis ring.

I'd tried very hard to pretend I was reformed but she didn't believe me. She was right, I was going along with her demands until she got bored of this game. She wasn't bored yet and was escalating the situation. I had to continue with her ridiculous ideas or lose my job and home. Feminised and humiliated or living on the street and begging and still feminised. I had to grit my teeth and pretend to accept it. It had to end soon, she couldn't keep this going.

Julie stopped dabbing my foreskin, which was a shame as it was the first tenderness I'd had for some time despite the humiliation of the circumstances. She checked my new pierced ears and wiped them with a piece of cotton wool. I pulled my dress over my erection. The damned bell tinkled twice as the dress touched the end of my penis.

Julie and Melissa stared at me. Something was going on. They had something to say. Julie went to speak, then stopped herself and put a finger over her thin lips. She looked at her knees. Whatever it was they were going to tell me wasn't going to be good news for me.

"Joanne." Melissa wasn't so timid. "You're going to spend some time away from working at the office."

I perked up. That wasn't such bad news. This was extremely good news. For the past week, I'd been steadily feminised and humiliated by Melissa at work with the other two ladies who worked there. I thought things were going to improve; my joy was to be short-lived.

"You're going to come and live with me for a while," said Melissa. The smile left my face like ice cream melting in the midday sun.

I couldn't see Julie's expression as her face remained looking down.

"Julie? What's this about?" I was desperate. This was a disaster.

Julie looked up, her hands held together on her knees. Her wide trousers provided a stark contrast to my short yellow dress. Things were the wrong way round, I should be in the trousers.

"We thought it for the best Joseph..., I mean Joanne," Julie said.

My mouth went as dry as a desert dune.

Melissa explained. "You now require specific and focused training, Joanne. We saw the need today when the ladies in the beauty parlour recognised you as a male."

I continued to look at Julie for an explanation. What did she mean by specific focussed training?

"I've behaved and done everything you asked, Julie. I've been humiliated by having to wear female clothing and endure the horrible penis ring and earrings. I'm a changed man. Please. When can I go back to normal and wear male clothing again?"

Melissa answered. "We don't believe you've learnt any lessons about your behaviour. In truth, Joanne, you have some way to go before I can say you are a changed character."

Melissa's comments cut through me. And she'd seen through me. I was playing the part they expected.

"Just shaving your body and wearing female clothing doesn't turn you into what I want you to be. We call this petticoat punishment and, for some males, it's sufficient and works well. In my experience, it works better on younger males. You're too set in your ways and need to experience a whole range of changes before we can say you're ready to be released back into the world."

I sat up straight and hard. "What do you mean released? When am I going to be able to dress as a man again?"

"When I release you from my control, Joanne, it will depend entirely on how quickly you learn from the intensive training programme you'll undergo at my house."

"So I just need to do your training course and then I can go back to male-hood?"

"Once you've undergone the transformations, and you've taken on the training and re-education, then I'll release you back to Julie." Melissa didn't blink. She stood up and gestured to me. "Now Joanne. We're leaving now. You're going to be spending a few weeks with me."

I had a nasty feeling those weeks were going to be extremely challenging.

3 The New Reality

I stared out of the bedroom window and out to the long garden of lawn and bushes. Melissa's house was an enormous Edwardian home with six bedrooms, one assigned to me on the first floor. I slouched on the bed, my foreskin felt sore from the piercing yesterday. Melissa locked the pink silicone chastity cage back on and hooked the cat's collar bell onto the bottom end of the cage and clicked its ring closed.

"I expect you will live here for at least the next six weeks. In my experience, this is the minimum time required to correct male behaviours and retrain and re-educate you."

This was not the first time she'd said, 'In my experience.' I did not like that idea one bit. I couldn't imagine a woman who'd forced men to submit to them and wear female clothing. Her words suggested I wasn't the first she'd worked on.

I wore a white summer dress that was short and hung loosely across my smooth shaved legs. They looked for all the world like girl's legs, even if my looks betrayed my real gender behind the girls' hair and clothes. I kicked off my high-heeled shoes and rubbed my aching calves.

"I'll leave you to get accustomed to your new environment for a few minutes, Joanne. Then we'll start work." She left before I could react.

Outside my new bedroom window, the unseasonably warm weather was broken by heavy rain. The skies were black and the rain pummelled against the window and the paving stones on the patio below.

Although still early evening, it was dark thanks to the storm. The gloom did not hide the bright pink walls of the bedroom. Everything was pink: the bedsheets, the pillows with a large frill, the tasselled lampshade and the bed covers. The floor was polished natural wood and I was surprised she hadn't had that painted pink too.

The house was in one of the wealthiest areas in the city. Melissa had serious money as the owner of her law firm. Thankfully I wasn't going to have to work there again for a while and maybe this 'retraining' would be less stressful.

The smell of the paint from the light pink skirting boards and walls and the stiffness of the bedding explained a recent redecoration. The wardrobe was full of brand-new dresses and skirts in my size, the drawers had panties, bras and stockings still in their packets. Laid out on top of the bed were two short baby-doll nighties, both with a low front and short pleated skirts flowing out from the chest. They wouldn't cover my panties. One was in powder pink and the other in ivory. Melissa had no plan to allow me to revert to any kind of masculinity while I was staying there, that was sure.

At that moment of self-reflection, Melissa popped her head around the door. "Come down to see me in the dining room in five minutes, Joanne." I heard her walking away from my room before I could answer.

I didn't want to upset her, the sooner I got through the next six weeks, the sooner I could get back to male-hood and my old life. I had to pretend harder that I was a reformed character. Sometimes you have to suffer to get what you want. I wanted a meek wife, her money and house and to be able to get back to regular trysts with a pretty girl or two or more. I was also dying for a few beers. That always made the evening swing.

The events of the past weeks made me think about my past behaviour for the first time. I did regret it but the trouble was I also enjoyed it. No responsibility and loads of fun. I'd planned to go along with Melissa's game of humiliate Joseph and then I could get back to life as normal.

I pulled up my dress to look at my humiliation of the cage, ring and the cat bell. I remembered the ring on the bell was not solid but had a gap. I pulled it apart and removed it. A small victory.

I slipped off the bed and made my way downstairs. I didn't bother with the high heels, they were too much trouble and too difficult to walk in. And they made my leg muscles ache. I wandered downstairs without the dreaded bell tinkling. I went into the dining room to see Melissa seated at the head of a dark wood oval dining table with two ladies sitting on either side of her and one standing. I'd not heard them and immediately stepped back to the door and stopped in the doorway as all eyes fell on me.

Standing behind Melissa with her hands together was a hard-faced girl in a plain black maid's uniform, like hotel cleaners wear. She looked about twenty-eight and attractive in a stern way. The lady to Melissa's right was tall and athletic. She wore her fair hair tied back in a small knot of a ponytail. She had chiselled cheekbones and muscular arms. She was a little older than the maid girl, about thirty-five years old. She was either a professional sportswoman or a fitness trainer although her erect manner also suggested military.

The lady on Melissa's right was different. She was smaller with masses of blond wavy hair that tumbled around her face. Her eyes were thick with black mascara and her eyelashes were far too long to be natural. She had a deeply tanned that didn't match her light hair and blue eyes. She tapped long fingernails of different patterns and colours on the tabletop. My eyes fixed on her enormous chest and low top. She was not an athlete like the other lady, that was sure. She would have had trouble running with those boobs.

The three ladies sitting at the table had glasses of white wine in front of them. They had been chatting but stopped when they saw me enter. They were comfortable with each other and clearly knew each other well.

Melissa sipped at her wine. "And here she is."

My face flushed hot at finding myself standing before them in the little summer dress.

Melissa's smile fell away. "Joanne, what have you forgotten?"

My eyes raised to the ceiling before I was able to stop them. It was a natural reaction to her comment, she spoke to me like I was a child. Melissa got up so swiftly that she was facing me before I could react. Her hand slapped across my cheek. My hand went to my face in shock. She'd slapped me with the others watching. The blonde lady's eyebrows arched but no one seemed shocked at what they'd seen.

"Joanne, you will never roll your eyes at me. If you do, your punishment will be much more severe than a slap around the face. Now, what have you forgotten, girl?"

My hand was still on my cheek and I instinctively cowered expecting another slap. It didn't come. "I, I don't know."

Melissa's hand were on her hips and she leaned forward into my face. I smelt her rich perfume and it was intoxicating. I marvelled at her change from her bland work clothing with knee-length skirts to the relaxed sexy clothing she had on outside work time. No one would have thought of her as the serious lawyer and company owner in the red minidress she now wore with her her air tousled and sexy.

"I'll help you this time, Joanne, as this is still new to you. Next time, I won't be so generous."

The blond lady sniggered into her hand.

"Curtsey."

I curtsied and my entire body burned with shame.

Melissa continued. "And I didn't hear the little bell when you came down the stairs. Would you like to tell me where it might be?" Melissa's tone had changed to a sneer.

My back arched as my usual anger built up. I forced it down, it would do no good. What would I achieve? I could exactly run away as all I had was a summer dress to wear and high-heeled shoes. I'm not going to get far in those. Besides I'd break Julie's agreement with

Melissa and there was only one outcome for that eventuality. Not a good prospect.

"It's upstairs in my bedroom, Melissa."

Whack! Melissa's hand slapped across my face again.

"It's upstairs in my bedroom, what?" I'd forgotten to call her Mistress.

I repeated the words using Mistress. That was stupid of me but I was flustered, especially being watched by those three unknown women. I turned to go and fetch the bell. Melissa retrained me with a firm hand on my arm.

"And what else have you forgotten, sissy girl?"

My body locked at hearing her call me sissy but I had the dress on so what was the problem now? My eyes fell on my bare feet. She was also looking at them. She wanted me in high heels.

"Yes," she said seeing where I was looking. "You should be wearing high heels all the time. You can only remove them for bed. You're going to have to learn to walk in them properly and that means constant practice."

I didn't like the sound of that. They weren't comfortable. Melissa released her grip and I scurried back to my new bedroom. I slipped on the high-heeled shoes and reattached the hated cat's bell to the bottom and end of the cage. I stood and immediately the bell tinkled. I stumbled back to the stairs, holding on to the bannister for support in my heels.

As I descended the steps, I was aware the ladies had stopped talking in the dining room. The silence accentuated the tinkling of the cat's bell on my foreskin on each step down the stairs in my ungainly way.

I saw the open door to the dining room off the large entrance hall and glanced at the front door. My whole body wanted to flee through it and escape this nightmare of humiliation. I should go back to Julie and plead for forgiveness. I'd tell her I'd never hurt her again. I'd say anything to revert to masculinity and this debasement of my manhood. But I had no money to get home and no male clothing.

I imagined the three-mile walk home from Melissa's house to ours in the little white dress. Julie wasn't about to take me back anyway so I'd face a shut door when I got there. I was trapped in Melissa's horror show and now she was introducing more of her associates who looked about to take part like Nina and Jane in the office did.

I lurched into the dining room where four pairs of eyes watched my every step. Melissa remained seated. "Stand at the end of the table, sissy girl."

I walked to the table and the bell tinkled on each step. The blond lady sniggered again.

"That's much better, Joanne," she said with a smug expression smeared across her face. Melissa continued. "We have a problem, Joanne sissy. It's obvious to everyone that you look like a man in girl's clothing. The way you walk, the way you hold yourself, your mannerisms. Although you're slim with long blond hair, your body and face are still too masculine. We're going to help you." Melissa ran an open hand out to introduce her colleagues.

I thought it best to remain silent. I looked down, trying to avoid the stares.

"You wouldn't want everyone thinking you're a man in a dress would you, Joanne? I'm sure you'd prefer to look like a pretty girl."

I wondered where she was going with this speech. I was certain I'd find out soon.

"We're going to help you blend in better." Melissa's face fell into a patronising smile "Any questions so far, Joanne?"

I only had one question and that was when she was going to release me from this torment and allow me to return to my old male life. I shook my head, my hair flowing from side to side across my face.

"After six weeks training and improvement with my two colleagues, we'll assess your progress. The process is all about re-educating and retraining you to become a much better person." Melissa sipped on her wine.

I wanted wine too, lots of it, but she wasn't about to offer me any. "So," I asked to make sure I understood. "After the six-week programme, you'll let me go and I can return to Julie?" I hoped but I had a bad feeling she'd make my time with her as difficult as possible.

"We'll see, Joanne."

I cringed at her use of the female name she'd given me.

"I will want to be sure you are a nice, well-behaved young lady before I let you go back to Julie."

I knew she was calling me a girl and dressing me feminine to humiliate me and make me see things from a female's perspective. I got that, even if I didn't like it. I was discomforted by her saying she wants me to be a well-behaved young *lady*. I shrugged it off. I guess she wants to continue to humiliate me by calling me a girl. OK, six weeks it is. It's not so long, is it?

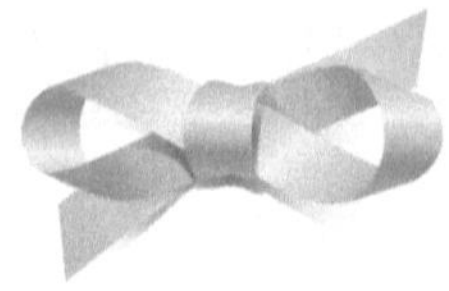

4 Tag Team

Melissa introduced the first of the ladies around her. She put a hand on a shoulder of the tall, imposing and athletic woman next to her. "This is Madam Imogen."

I avoided pulling a face at having to spend time with yet another female with a title. Mistress this, Madam that. Melissa was trying to grind me into the floor by making me address women as superiors.

Imogen didn't react and she watched me coldly. "Madam Imogen will be your personal coach. She will teach you how to behave, walk, and sit properly and also how to speak politely and demurely like a good girl."

Melissa reeled this list off as if it was normal behaviour to make a man into a sissy girl.

"She will also oversee your diet and fitness regime, Joanne."

I nodded my head from side to side in agreement. I didn't see a problem with being a little fitter, at least some good might out of this ridiculous charade of training.

Melissa spotted my acceptance of starting a training regime.

"Joanne," she spluttered, "do not think that fitness means building big masculine muscles. No, this regime will be about reshaping your body into something more appropriate. Slimmer and more refined."

This didn't concern me as a bit of physical activity was fine. As I was imagining weights and treadmills I imagined working out with Imogen. It might be fun. Imogen looked like she was sucking on battery acid when I looked at her. Maybe I could cheer her up a little with my famous chat-up lines. Once out of a dress and in male gym wear, I was confident she would see me as the cheeky chap who had been so successful with so many women in the past.

With her face still with disgust etched in it, Imogen spoke. "You will address me as Madam or Ma'am at all times," she said in a clipped military accent. "You will never mention my name, just my title. Madam. Ma'am. Do you understand me, girl?"

I nodded and noted her stiff formal speech style confirmed she was almost certainly ex-military. That might not be a good sign, I thought.

Melissa moved on to point to the blond lady. "Mandy will be your beauty stylist."

My body sagged at those words, remembering what happened the last time I went to a beautician. I fingered my earlobes to feel the large loop earrings in my pierced ears and felt the sensation of my pierced penis. I shuddered.

"Mandy is going to work on your hairstyle, makeup, personal hygiene, nails and areas like eyebrows, electrolysis and waxing. She will make you more feminine and pretty."

I shivered again although Mandy was the type of girl I'd had lots of success with in the past. I assumed she had less than average intelligence, I guessed. She was probably only interested in makeup and hair. I thought she may be around 34 years old. I might get somewhere with her, I reflected. More chance than with Imogen.

"Mandy is a businesswoman I met at the club and owns five beauty parlours across the city. You will address her as Ms Mandy."

I gulped. Mandy was not as dim as I'd thought. Appearances were deceptive. Mandy waved a delicate hand and called out a friendly, "Hi, Joanne, I'm looking forward to working with you, sweetie. We're going to have fun together, you're almost a blank canvas, can't wait." She squeezed her face up.

At least Mandy's smiling face was friendlier than Melissa's or Imogen's. That was something. As for fun, I only had one idea of fun and being feminised wasn't that.

Melissa asked the young maid girl who had been standing behind her to come around. She was short and slim and her figure boyish showed no perceptible hips or boobs. Her coal-black hair was pulled back harshly into a long ponytail.

"I Maja, Melissa housekeeper." She seemed to spit out the words in a strong accent.

"Maja is a financial graduate from Hungary," Melissa added. "She earns far more money as my housekeeper than as an accountant in Budapest. She'll return home in a year or two, once she'd saved up for a deposit for her first home back in Hungary. In the meantime, Maja will be teaching you how to clean, wash, cook, serve and any other household tasks that you will need as a sissy housemaid."

Sissy housemaid? What was that? I breathed out in exasperation. I hated housework. I suppose I will have to show some willingness in this area once I went back to Julie.

"Maja, you may leave us for now," said Melissa. "For the first few days, Imogen and Mandy have a few priorities to deal with regarding Joanne's looks and manner before we get onto maid duties."

Maja nodded solemnly, glared at me for a moment, and left the room

Melissa clapped her hands together and I jumped. "Time for bed, Joanne, you've got a big day tomorrow. Imogen will take you upstairs and begin preparations."

It was only 6.30 in the evening. My eyes swivelled to Imogen and the tall impassive lady stood up from the table and moved over to me.

"Upstairs, girl."

It was beginning.

5 Foam Bath Time

I wasn't too concerned it was so early. I felt tired and wanted to get away from the group of women. I went to my new bedroom and sat on the bed. smoothing out my dress over my legs. It was light and sensual and I was pleased to enjoy these sensations alone.

After several minutes of enjoying my quiet contemplation, Imogen came into the room. I hadn't heard her. She was carrying a dark piece of polished wood like a small paddle. It was thin and around 18 inches long and about five inches wide at one end. She held the narrow handle down her leg and tapped it menacingly against her thigh. She strode in and waited at the end of my single bed. Her legs were splayed apart and she raised the wooden device and tapped it in her other hand while raising a single eyebrow. This did not look good.

Imogen was probably over six feet tall with defined, lean muscles. She wore tight dark blue jeans tucked into high black boots that went over her knee at the front. They had a low heel, I guessed because of her height. Her cream-coloured v-neck pullover was as tight fitting as her jeans. Her broad shoulders were more like a man's and I guessed she was a swimmer or weight lifter. She'd released her hair from the ponytail she had in downstairs and it now hung straight a couple of inches above her shoulders. Her face radiated pure health and I saw no wrinkles or blemishes and little makeup.

"Remove your clothes, girl." She continued to tap the wooden paddle-like stick in her hand which was increasingly threatening. A key swung on a light chain around her neck, I guessed it was the key to my chastity cage. In different circumstances, I would have happily stripped off for someone so sexy although she would not have been my first choice. Too damn arrogant.

I guessed I'd have to do as she ordered as I assumed the paddle device was intended for intimidation and use. I had no doubt she'd use it and, with those muscles in her arms, it was sure to be painful.

I stood and pulled off my dress over my head. I unhooked the bra and let it and the breast forms fall to the floor. My eyes met hers in my small act of defiance. Imogen's expression turned to exaggerated boredom and she shrugged her shoulders. She slipped the paddle stick under her arm and unlocked my chastity cage. My penis burst free and grew like a long balloon receiving an injection of compressed air. The Albert ring glinted from a ray of the fading summer light through the window. A thought shot through my brain that Imogen was so uptight she needed someone like me to give her a good fucking. The old Joseph's thoughts fell away like an autumn leaf in the wind. The male-female power balance was firmly the other way these days.

Imogen's mouth raised at the corner in a half smile but there was no warmth in her eyes. She tapped the stick in her hand again. "Whenever you do as I say, girl, everything will be fine for you. The second you disobey me or talk back you will feel the force of my wooden paddle against your scrawny arse."

I looked down, there was nothing to say to that statement, she held all the cards including strength and size.

She moved in closer to me and I smelt a light perfume or maybe scented soap. "You will answer me, yes Ma'am."

"Yes, Ma'am." It was easier that way but I felt the rebel inside stirring.

Maja came into the room at that moment and my body sagged. How many more women were going to be present at my humiliations? Maja stared at my penis ring for an uncomfortable time. I went to pull my hands over my erection. Maja held a tray with what looked like an aluminium dog's bowl on it with slices of chicken and green vegetables in it. There was a dessert spoon alongside it. Maja wore a white full-length plastic apron over her black maid dress. It was the type of apron that nurses wear when they are about to do something in a hospital that may be messy. She pulled her eyes away from my penis ring.

"Here is dinner, Joanne."

Her hard accent grated on my frayed nerves and spoke every word as if it were a separate sentence. Melissa was turning the screw and feeding me food from a dog's bowl. I was thankful they had supplied a spoon at least. I wasn't hungry, I felt sick. Or was that excitement? Something in my subconscious mind was enjoying these humiliations. Even Maja's stern boyish features carried a certain charm in this humiliating environment I'd been forced into. I knew it was my fault but I had never expected this type of retaliation.

"If you're not hungry that's good. You need to reduce your stomach size by a few inches." Imogen had resumed tapping her paddle in one hand. It was aggressive.

"I have a 32-inch waist, Ma'am." I was slim without an ounce of fat.

Imogen was not impressed. "That's a man's size. When you're at a feminine 24 inches, then I'll be satisfied."

24 inches; that was insane. I was sure she was being deliberately antagonistic.

Maja placed the tray with the dog's bowl on a side unit and approached me. "Bath time, Joanne."

"Every morning and every night you will shower or bath. We want you to smell sweet and fragrant, Joanne," said Imogen. "Like the pretty sissy girl you're becoming."

Maja grasped my erection and pulled me firmly towards the door, as if it were a dog's lead. Imogen followed, her paddle menacingly held down along the side of her leg. Disturbingly, she was tapping her leg again with it, as if she were looking for a reason to use it on me at the slightest excuse.

We went onto the landing and across to the bathroom. As we approached the open bathroom door, the smell of flowery fragrance became stronger; it floated in the air. Once I went into the bathroom, the smell was overpowering.

Maja pulled me in firmly by my erection. "Maja, don't pull so hard, you'll hurt my cock."

Thwack, it was the excuse Imogen was looking for. A sharp pain stung my bare buttocks. Thwack, a second hit and tears welled in my eyes. It stung but my tears were more from the humiliation.

"Never tell a lady what or what not to do," said Imogen and I rubbed my sore bottom cheeks. "Never address any lady without using their title. It's *Miss* Maja. Do you understand me, girl?" Imogen had the paddle at shoulder height ready to fall on my behind again. I had to give in and quickly.

"Yes Madam Imogen, sorry Madam Imogen, I won't do it again." I hoped my submission would stop her from spanking me with the paddle.

Imogen lowered the dreaded paddle to her side as I cowered. She started the annoying leg tapping once again. Better the leg tapping than using it on me.

I saw that Maja had run a bath. It overflowed with foam and bubbles. She pointed to it and now I saw the reason for Maja's plastic apron.

"Keep arms out of water and bubbles and in air," she said.

"Why," I asked.

"So we see you not touch clitty. Mistress Melissa say not allowed. Joanne not touch her clitty."

"How will I wash it then?"

Imogen answered for her. "I told you to never question a lady, sissy. As Maja explained, you are not allowed to touch yourself ever. So Maja will wash your girly bits, hence the apron and latex gloves. Get in and hold your arms up."

My mouth dropped open as if a heavy weight were suddenly attached to it. I stepped into the warm bath. I raised my arms as Imogen had ordered, mindful of the tapping paddle in her hand.

Maja slapped on a pair of white latex medical gloves like a doctor about to perform a nasty procedure. She rubbed soap into a flannel. She rubbed it all around my genitals and I nearly fainted. She pulled back my partially withdrawn foreskin and washed the head of my penis with the flannel, making my eyes water. She then scrubbed all around my scrotum. Her nose was screwed up in distaste the whole time, keeping her head back and to one side as if I had a nasty smell. It was excruciatingly mortifying to be treated this way. She scrubbed the tops of my legs and motioned for me to sit down by lowering her hand.

"Wash body, Joanne. Keep arms out of foam and water," she said.

I scrubbed my upper body and face with a sponge full of foam and suds under the disinterested eye of Imogen and Maja's scowl. I could see Imogen saw this as her role in my emasculation and Maja would have preferred to be elsewhere. I wondered if Melissa had told her she'd be cleaning a naked man's penis and balls in a foam bath when she took her on.

Once I had washed, I stepped out of the suds and into a floor towel. Maja passed me an enormous pink fluffy towel to dry myself. We returned to my bedroom, me naked behind Maja with Imogen following and towering over me. The scent from the oils and perfumes in the water had soaked into every pore of my skin and I walked in a curtain of my feminine perfumes.

We returned to my pink bedroom. Imogen clipped on my chastity cage and held up the pink baby-doll nightie. Maja sniggered and held a hand over her mouth.

I slipped the nightie over my head as Imogen tapped her thigh with the paddle. The nightie was light and short and the frilly hem rested against the top of the pink cage. Imogen placed the cat's bell on the bedside cabinet.

My nightie was elasticated under my chest and had two lacy straps over my shoulders. The front was low cut. The skirt part flared out from the chest area in small pleats to hang on the top of the pink cage. The soft feel of the chiffon was delicate and intoxicating against my smooth body. I'd never felt anything so feminine and I hated how wonderful it was. My penis strained against the silicon cage, my erection skin against the open slits but had nowhere to go. My balls were bursting with desperation and wanted to explode. This desperation stung my lower stomach. I was not going to get any relief. I gritted my teeth.

Imogen had one more order. "Every night after your bath and once you have your nightdress on, you will go down to wish Mistress Melissa goodnight. You will curtsey to her and then return to bed. Let's go."

This couldn't be happening. Maja scurried from the room, she was doing what she'd been paid for and now wanted to go. Imogen was also on Melissa's pay, but she was a different proposition revelling in her role as my feminisation tutor. She grabbed my arm and led me downstairs and into Melissa's large front room.

A square bay window looked out onto a front garden full of low bushes and mature trees. Light blue velvet floor-to-ceiling curtains were drawn. Melissa sat in an armchair. She was wearing glasses and reading typed papers that I assumed to be legal documents. She looked up as we entered. Her long tussled hair hung over her shoulder and her short dress rode up high on firm strong thighs. She peered over the top of her reading spectacles.

I curtsied by holding each side of my nightie, my cock cage exposed and protruding. "Goodnight, Mistress Melissa," I said as instructed by Imogen who stood by me like a prison guard.

Melissa smiled sweetly, the first time I'd seen a gentle side of her when dealing with me. "Good girl Joanne, now off to bed with you. A busy first full day of improvement work awaits you tomorrow. I'm certain this is going to work out well and you're going to become such a pretty well-behaved girl." She looked down at her papers and ignored me any further.

Imogen took my arm. I didn't like Melissa saying I was to be a girl. I knew it was to humiliate me but it didn't stop me worrying. I understood that she was humiliating me and teaching me how a female sees the world but I'd eventually be a man again. It was some kind of perverted revenge for my treatment of Julie. I accepted that to some degree as I had no choice. I also accepted that I had behaved badly, but I was not about to become a girl. It had to be part of the game she was playing. A psychological game.

6 A Girl's Morning Rituals

I had a bad night's sleep. How did they expect me to sleep well when my cock was squashed inside a tight cage and my nightie twisted around my body? I wondered how women wear these baby dolls.

I thumped at the mattress with a fist. It wasn't just the cock cage and nightie, it was the whole experience of being trapped here and humiliated. I had to find a way to speak to Julie. I was sure if she knew exactly what was going on, she'd put a stop to Melissa's feminisation and submission games. It was one thing to put me in girlie clothes to teach me a lesson but another to put me through this abject ignominy. And Imogen with the paddle was a step too far. It was as if I was in a prison and she was the guard. Julie wouldn't like that surely. Even though she was timid, she'd speak to Melissa for me. Even timid people have their limits.

I thought for a few moments about taking the baby-doll nightie off. That was probably not a good idea. Imogen would not like that. Even without the wooden paddle she carried, she was far more powerful than me.

I spotted a pink young girl's alarm clock by my bed for the first time. It had a cartoon kitty on the white face behind wide black hands. Melissa was using every trick to make me feel girly and feminine. Not just feminine, but like a young girl. The clock said 7 am. At that moment Imogen strode in, her knee-high black boots making a dull thudding on the wooden floor. Maja followed her wearing the white plastic apron, latex gloves and a wide grimace.

"Time to get up and showered, girl," Imogen called like the parade ground sergeant I imagined her to be. Today, she had a riding crop tucked under her arm.

I went to the bathroom and she pointed to the glass cubicle shower. After showering with my cage on, watched by Imogen without expression and Maja yawning, I got out of the shower.

Imogen unlocked my chastity cage and held it out to me. "Wash it out in the sink, girl," she said.

I washed it under running water and using soap gel. I placed it next to the taps and put my hands over my penis. I was fed up with being naked under their glare. Imogen spotted my movement and tapped both arms with her riding drop.

"Hands by your side, girl, and away from clitty. No touching clitty." Imogen raised an eyebrow.

I had the feeling of a being soldier on a parade ground with Sergeant-Major Imogen as my drill instructor. Maja collected a small sponge and tipped some shower gel into it and rinsed it under the cold tap. She rubbed it on my penis which sprung to attention as I squealed at the cold. She cleaned under the foreskin again and around my balls and anus.

"This silly little thing. Like baby worm." She scowled at me.

She rinsed me off and dried me as I squeezed my whole bottom cheeks together trying not to cum. It had been so long and I was so desperate that even Maja's less-than-delicate penis and ball scrubbing had an erotic effect. Or maybe because of it

Back in my bedroom, Imogen placed my chastity cage on the top of the side cabinet. She clipped the cat's bell to my penis ring. I wondered what the day had in store for me. It didn't bode well.

Maja passed me a bottle of white moisturiser cream. "Rub in legs. Is pretty girl cream. Smell pretty."

I rubbed it in under their gaze, the horrible bell tinkled as I moved. rubbed in. Maja then sprayed a strong flowery perfume over my face and neck. She passed me a brush and I used it to comb through my long thick hair which draped over my shoulders. It was getting long.

"Shoes." Imogen pointed to my four-inch high heels. I walked over and slipped into them and stood unsteadily.

Imogen went to the wardrobe, flung open the doors and stepped back as Maja opened the curtains. A bright sunny morning greeted me. I wanted to be outside, in the garden, wearing male clothes and free. Instead, I was naked in high-heeled shoes with a cat's bell hanging from the end of my erection.

I looked out at the mature bushes and trees in the long front garden and through the waist-high metal gate to the quiet lane. The day outside was promising but the day inside was not.

Tap tap. Imogen's crop banged on the wardrobe door to bring me out of my daydream. "Put this on after you've put your bra on and breast forms in."

Imogen's crop touched a short light rose pink summer dress. Lace frills ran along the hem. A low-cut front and short sleeves were also capped with white lace. The shoulders had two puffy frills. After putting on my bra under Imogen's gaze and the breast forms, I slipped the dress on over my head. The soft light cotton dress hugged my body around my chest. The short dress hung light to the top of my thighs and was no more than a whisker below my penis end. It was going to be a hot summer's day and the dress would be perfect for such a day if I'd been a young girl. I wasn't. I was a 45-year-old man.

The feel of the material against my body and the rubbing of the soft material on my penis head was excruciating and sensual. My erection grew hard and firm. I looked down in despair as the bell and penis ring pushed below the hem of my dress and pushed it up. My shaft and balls were now fully exposed. Imogen watched without emotion for a few moments. She then used her crop to push the dress hem up the erect stem of my penis. It stayed there laying on top of my cage.

"Breakfast. Now. In the dining room." Imogen marched out of the room waving her crop to tell me to follow.

In the dining room, Melissa was already seated at the head of the table with Mandy on her left. The bell tinkled as entered the room. With my erection fully exposed, it hung free to ring as I walked. Maja came into the room on hearing the bell and carried the dog's bowl with muesli and milk in it and a spoon. She placed it on the floor by Melissa's feet.

"Sit on the floor by me for your breakfast, there's a good girl." Melissa had ramped her domination over me up several notches.

Without looking at me, Melissa continued talking as I curtsied and sat on the floor by her feet. My erection pointed to the ceiling although Melissa appeared uninterested. "This morning, Joanne, Mandy is going to start work on you."

She didn't add what exactly Mandy would be doing but my stomach fluttered.

Melissa looked down and saw my strong erection.

"I see you like that idea, Joanne. That's good. She'll make you a pretty girl."

My stomach turned over in panic. At the same time, the problem of my quick temper emerged inside me. My face reddened and I tightened my mouth to avoid saying anything as I would have in the past. It was a past when I was a real male and not a weak sissy sitting on the floor at the feet of a dominant woman with absolute power over me. It was oddly exciting. I pushed that idea away. I didn't want to become a sissy girl and I had to put my foot down before Melissa got the impression I did.

I stood, huffing. "Mistress Melissa, I understand why you're doing this to me. I know my past behaviour was not good. I'm now a reformed character. Play your humiliation game for the next six weeks but I can never become a pretty girl. I'm a man and after six weeks, I'm going to return to being a man. I'll go home to Julie after this is over and find a good job and be a real man and husband for her. I promise." There it was, out and I'd said it. That would put her straight about how things were going to be. I sat back down feeling silly I'd given my speech with my erect penis on show with a bell on the end.

I waited for a reply. Nothing. Melissa buttered a slice of toast and Mandy asked Imogen to pass the jam. Silence. I couldn't stop myself, I had to speak again. "Mistress? Did you hear me?"

Melissa cut her toast and took a bite. More silence. She looked across the table at Imogen. "When you've finished your breakfast, Imy, you may give Joanne my reply."

Imogen nodded with a sparkle in her eyes.

Imogen finished eating her toast and sipped on a glass of orange juice. She then stood up, taking her riding crop in one hand. She lifted the palm of her free hand to show me that she wanted me to get up again.

I stood and pulled the hem of my dress down over my penis which was a wasted effort as it popped out again. The dress was far too short and my penis was too hard to remain under the tiny piece of a skirt of the dress.

"Lift your dress to your stomach, girl." Imogen's order was followed by her lifting my dress with her riding crop. I took it and held it to my stomach, my penis poked out hard and firm.

Whack. Imogen's crop came down on the exposed shaft. I pulled back but Imogen's expression told me to go back to the same position. Whack again across the top of my erection. It stung and the stinging persisted, throbbing. Another three swipes of her crop came down on my reddening erect shaft. Stinging pain and stinging pleasure.

Melissa did not look at me but said after taking a sip of orange juice, "You will never question any woman, ever. I may do whatever I please with you, Joanne. Julie has handed you to me for correction and the methods with which I correct you are entirely my decision. For the duration of your stay with me, you will be a full-time submissive girl.

Until you look and act like a pretty submissive sissy, you will remain here. Only once you have become a well-behaved and polite young lady will I release you back into the world again."

I gasped at the enormity of what she'd said. I had to pass as a girl or I couldn't be released back to Julie. I think that's what she meant. Panic hit me. "Mistress, I can never be a girl."

"You don't think so, Joanne? You're already on that road. I've found it to be the only way to correct poor male behaviour. Sissyfication and feminisation. It works every time."

I gave out a gasp but Melissa hadn't finished. "Now, Joanne, I know you used to be a male and males have problems remembering things. So, I've printed out my rules for you to pin up on your bedroom wall. They will help you remember. These rules are absolute. Any failure to follow them to the letter will result in punishment. You've already experienced the paddle and crop so I'm sure you won't want that."

I shook my head like a naughty schoolboy. Or was that schoolgirl? Melissa handed me the paper and she told me to read the rules out loud. I cleared my throat and read silently. I could not believe what I saw printed. This had to be a joke.

7 Mistress's House Rules

I cleared my throat again. "We're waiting," said Melissa. This is what I read.

The Ten House Rules for Sissies.

One. A sissy must obey any woman at any time in any situation without question. Instructions must be followed instantly. You will thank the lady after receiving your instructions, whatever they might be.

Two. All women will be addressed with a title to signify their superiority over sissy. This will be Mistress by default but sissy will use whatever title the lady in question demands.

Three. Sissies must wear only girl's clothes or present naked. Trousers are not permitted under any circumstances even if female.

Four. Sissies are not permitted to touch their clitties or pussies. When alone, they will wear a clitty chastity cage to prevent any risk. Sissies are weak and cannot be trusted.

Five. When a sissy clitty is released from a cage, they will not be permitted to wear underwear.

Six. Sissies will wear a cat bell attached to their clitties or chastity cages unless instructed otherwise by a female. It's sissy's responsibility to ensure it is attached.

Seven. Sissies will curtsey to all women whenever you enter or leave a room, perform a task for them, receive punishment or after receiving instructions.

Eight. Sissies must be polite and deferential at all times to all women.

Nine. Sissies must wear high-heeled shoes at all times. A minimum height of four inches is expected although up to six inches will be required at times on the Mistress's orders.

Ten. Sissies are not permitted to use chairs or stools unless given specific permission by a lady. Sissies will sit on the floor at all times, if permitted to sit.

"These rules are in effect from now, sissy. You will follow them or face the consequences." Melissa sat back.

I held the paper with the rules on feeling worried. Melissa stood and picked up a briefcase. She was leaving for the office. "I can see you're a little surprised but the rules are the rules and you are already used to some of them. We'll start with you curtseying to me and thanking me for taking the time to provide the rules for you."

I swallowed hard, but had no choice. I took the hem of my short dress and bent my knee to curtsey. I bowed my head and mumbled, "Thank you, Mistress."

"Excellent," Melissa laughed. "Imogen I think sissy needs some work on how to curtsey properly."

"Yes, Mel," Imogen replied.

Melissa left the room and a second later the front door slammed behind her with a heavy thud.

Imogen thought for a long moment. "Today, girl, we're going to make you look prettier. You'll be in Mandy's excellent hands all morning." She turned to Mandy. I'll leave you to it, Mands. Any problems with her, let me know." She left the room and it was as if a heavy dark cloud went with her.

As Maja cleared the table, Mandy's face opened into a sunny smile. She put two manicured hands together as if she were about to pray. Her long nails were perfect and multi-coloured. Her platinum blond hair was thick and wavy and tumbled over her narrow shoulders to halfway down her small back. She stood and her white satin blouse looked about to burst such was the tightness across her enormous bosoms.

My eyes fell on her cleavage then down to a short white pencil skirt, no more than eight inches long. Old habits died hard. I hoped they wouldn't try to put me in something similar as it would never cover my flaccid penis let alone if it got hard. That was almost a permanent condition recently.

Mandy tugged on the hem of her skirt and led me down to the basement via a spiral staircase below the main stairs to the floors above. Unlike the taciturn Imogen, Mandy didn't stop chatting as we went downstairs. She even answered her own questions, "Do you like being a cute sissy? Oh, I can see you do, dearie. I imagine you love the cute girly clothes, don't you? Yes, of course you do, all sissies love them, they just pretend not to."

My tinkling penis bell mingled with her high-pitched London-accented chatter as we descended the basement stairs. I did not understand how you would know that all sissies loved wearing girls' clothes. I'd gone from one extreme to the other as Mandy treated me as a captive audience to her incessant chat. By the time we'd reached a private basement beauty parlour, my head was thumping.

If this wasn't bad enough, she thought the idea of my feminisation was, "Cute," as she kept saying. That was her favourite word – *Cute.* She had a vocabulary all of her own. She told me my penis bell was '*well-cute*'. Was '*well cute*' proper English? She asked me if I liked the bell and then told me I must do before I could answer. She said it was *so cute,* I must love it too.

She told me she liked the way the lace of my little white dress hem lay on my, *'Cute tinky'*. *Tinky*, I discovered, was her word for a penis and another word in the Mandy book of unique baby-type vocabulary. She took a breath and there was a moment of silence. She then filled the silence telling me how pretty my little dress was. So feminine and girly. And cute, of course. She wanted to know if I liked my, *"Cute dressy-wessy'*? *'Dressy-wessy?'* My head whorled around like a boat rotating in a violent whirlpool.

She guided me to a large leather reclining hairdresser chair as Mandy wittered on about hairdressing, nail extensions and false eyelashes. It was only then I realised she was talking about what she was going to do to me. "What exactly do you have planned, Mandy?"

She wagged a long painted nail at me and tutted. "Miss Mandy, did you not listen to Melissa's rules?" She giggled a moment and said to herself, "Sissies, they are silly billies."

"Miss Mandy," I corrected myself. And silly-billies? I hadn't heard that expression since I was six. For the first time, there was a moment's silence as her face went from a permanent grin to a serious look.

"Melissa wants you to look more girly and that is what I'm going to do to you. I know that as a sissy, you'll pretend to complain but that's all part of the game, isn't it Joanne."

It always came down to what Melissa wanted. And Melissa seemed to like men feminised. I was getting the feeling I was not the first to pass through here by any means.

There was a moment's silence as Mandy prepared. "Joanne darling, I have Melissa's instructions and you have to allow me to work." She looked at me closely. Her perfume was overpowering and her makeup was over-applied. "We don't want sissy-wissy playing pretend-not-to-want-to-be-a-girly, do we, honey?"

I wasn't entirely sure what she was babbling about.

She tapped me on the nose. "And if missy-sissy plays up, I'll have to call Imogen and *we wouldn't want that, would we?* We're going to have such a lovely girly time together, making you look so pretty... and cute."

I wondered when she'd mention that word again.

"OK, Miss Mandy, get on with whatever you have to do. The sooner I look the way Melissa wants, the sooner I get to the stage where I can get back to being a man again.

Mandy looked genuinely surprised. "A man? Why ever would you want that?"

"Yes," I said angrily. "A man."

Mandy stopped her constant blur of excited movement for a moment. "Melissa said you wanted to be a girl, as sissy as possible. That's what I'll be doing today, darling."

"No Mandy, I don't want to be a girl. This is my punishment as Melissa thinks I've misbehaved. Once she's humiliated me enough, I can go back to my wife and return to being a man again."

Mandy gawped at me, her mouth open. Then she laughed out loud, a sound not unlike a donkey's bray. "You are a joker, Joanne dearie." She looked relieved at what she thought had happened and continued her monologue. "So, dearie, first I'm going to work on your hair. It's nice and long and I'm going to colour it, give it some curl and some cute waves and make it much thicker in appearance. Much cuter. And prettier."

I sighed.

"While your hair is setting and colouring, I'm going to do your fingers and toenails with pink-coloured shellac. It's longer lasting than varnish and I'll fit nail extensions. Melissa wants bright pink so pink it is but I think it's a good choice for you. We know how much sissies love pink."

I slumped at the thought of pink nails.

"Then," she continued seemingly without breathing, "I'm going to fit false eyelashes, thin your eyebrows out and make your face up properly."

"OK, Mandy, I suppose I have no choice."

She thumped me on the arm and told me I was a joker. "Then tomorrow, I'll work on your body hair problem. "And don't let Imogen hear you call me Mandy. Miss Mandy remember?"

I sat up registering her comment. "What body hair problem?"

She punched me again on my arm and told me again I was, *"Such a cute sissy she wants to squeeze me up."*

Despite her childish manner, being with Mandy far better than being with Imogen. I guessed I might as well relax and accept I could do nothing about what she had been told to do to me. I was tired from lack of sleep so I closed my eyes and allowed her to work on me.

She began on my hair and it made a pleasant change to have someone being nice to me after Melissa's aggressive behaviour, Julie's indifference and then Imogen. Mandy washed my hair as I lay backwards over a sink and pulled me up in the chair. Her constant talking droned in my head, like a wasp bashing against a window pane. The droning receded into the back of my brain. I must have fallen deeply asleep as I was woken by Mandy shaking me. I sat up sharply, pretending I hadn't been asleep. I blinked at my hands and held them up to my sleepy eyes. My nails were a quarter of an inch long and a luminous pink.

"What happened?" was all I could manage to say.

"Do you like them, sissy darling?" Mandy enquired, seemingly wanting approval. "They are false acrylic nails that I glued on. You can keep them on until your nails grow and become strong enough."

I didn't reply as I was still in shock. Mandy pointed to my feet. I looked past my short dress and to my toes. They were the same shade of pink and with a white tip. Mandy had shaped them too.

"Cute, no?" she said, not unexpectedly.

"Yes, I know, cute."A strong tone of sarcasm ran through my voice.

"Yeah, cute," she said with a smile.

She hadn't picked up my sarcasm or perhaps ignored it. My eyes went to the mirror above the sink opposite me. What had she done to my hair? It was blond. Waves flowed and fell over my shoulders and down my front and back. I puffed at my fringe with a thumb and finger as it was falling into my eyes. I then spotted the other change. I was in full makeup. There was so much to see I was unable to take it all in. My eyelashes looked odd. I put my face closer to the mirror. She had attached long black false lashes. I blinked.

"I've given you a fringe and backcombed and blow-dried your hair to make it look bigger and thicker. I pulled it into your face. That's to disguise your slightly masculine face. I'm sure you'll be much prettier once you've gone through Imogen's regime." Mandy giggled. Her eyes were not on my face but lower down.

My penis had grown again at my look and poked up below the dress. Why was I so excited to be feminised? I hated and loved it at the same time. It felt too wonderful. I hated myself for my excitement.

Mandy gazed at my erection as if in a daze, head on one side. "Tinky's excited. How sweet. That's so cute. Sissies always love being made up like this."

I swore that if she said the word cute again, I would scream. She moved down to look closer which only increased the strength of my erection. She lifted the dress to see. She touched the end lightly to make the bell tinkle. She put her hand to her mouth and giggled again. She held my erection between two fingers and jingled the bell several times, giggling each time. My body burned with embarrassment.

The door to the room swung open and Imogen marched in; march being the perfect verb to describe my personal sergeant major's style of walking. After saying hello to Mandy and kissing her on both cheeks, she walked around my chair inspecting me, mumbling something.

Imogen looked up at Mandy. "Nice work Mandy. Did she behave herself?"

Mandy nodded in response, her mane of blond hair moving as one with her head. "Yes, she was a good sissy girl '*Imy*'. No problems." She finished spraying my hair, putting the hairspray down with a clunk.

I looked again in the mirror and I was looking very different. To be blunt, I looked like a girl. At the same time, there was something in my face that would still make someone look twice if they were close up. Something that said there was a man hidden under the makeup and mop of hair. That was a relief for me. When this period of humiliation ended I expected to go back to masculinity. I'd start with a haircut. A buzz cut sounded like a good start.

Imogen tapped me with her riding crop. "Girl. We're going to have lunch and then we'll start your afternoon lessons on female deportment, posture, behaviour and manners. Thank Miss Mandy for making you look more girly. You'll be back tomorrow for work on your body hair. We can't have a pretty girl like you with any nasty male body hair can we?"

As I curtsied and thanked a giggling Mandy for making me prettier, I wondered what she meant by hair removal. I'd been on a regime of hair removal by shaving my legs, chest and pubic hair for a couple of weeks. What more could I do?

For now, my concern was spending an afternoon with Imogen. She slapped her riding crop against her boot and we left. This could only go downhill.

8 High heels and voice

My legs and my feet were killing me. After lunch, Imogen made me walk up and down the living room for ages. To the wall, then back. Fifty times? A hundred times? I'd lost count. She said she wanted me to walk properly in my high-heeled shoes. Like a proper girl.

"Please, Ma'am, can I start in lower heels, maybe two inches? It would help me to get more used to heels."

She scoffed. "No, girl. All the shoes we have for you are a minimum four-inch heel. Some are six inches high. You start in four and move up to six. Not two to four. That's ridiculous. You're to become a sissy, not a lady."

Four inches it was, I had no choice. My calves were complaining and they were as tight as piano wire.

After an hour of this, Imogen allowed me a five-minute rest and a glass of water. Water was the only liquid intake I was to be permitted for the next six weeks. Absolutely no alcohol, too many carbs she said. I missed this.

Imogen made me stand on floor scales. "You're far too heavy, girl. 11 stone, 154 pounds. We want you closer to 10 stone, 140 pounds. Like a slim demure sissy girl."

That was skinny for a man of five foot nine. I was on a strict diet. Apart from water, it was salads only and no carbs such as rice, pasta, potatoes or bread. I was hungry.

Imogen motioned for me to start walking again. I walked up and down for the rest of the afternoon, small steps, head up, chest out. "Walk like a girl," she said. "Soon I'll teach you female bottom, hip and arm movements to the way you walk. One step at a time," she said then looked perplexed at the idea she may have inadvertently made a pun.

The *clip-clop* of my heels and the *tinkle-tinkle* of my penis bell under my dress were playing in my head like one of those catchy tunes you can't stop humming. This wasn't catchy just repetitive – *clip-clop, tinkle-tinkle, clip-clop, tinkle-tinkle.* Up and down the wooden floor I strode in the damn heels.

After more than three hours, even Imogen accepted I was struggling. She allowed me to sit on a chair. I didn't say anything but I hoped this was a moment of weakness, of some humanity peeking through Imogen's tough exterior Melissa seemed to prefer that I sat on the floor.

My thoughts were dashed as I was about to see that sitting on a chair wasn't for my comfort but the start of a different type of training. Sitting down demurely like a delicate girl.

I began more repetition. Getting up and then sitting down on the chair, following Imogen's instructions on style and manner. At least my feet were able to recover a little although not my legs which were seizing up with the strain of standing in high heels and then letting myself down daintily.

After an hour and a half of this, Imogen ordered me to stop, curtsey and thank her for my training in feminine development.

I curtsied and said, "Thank you, Madam Imogen."

She growled, "You need lessons in curtseying, girl, you're far too clumsy".

I didn't care, I was pleased for the rest and to stop my light cotton dress rubbing against the end of my penis causing it to be permanently aroused. Sitting down and drinking water meant I could avoid the erotic cotton rubbing against the end. I hoped the erection would go down, it had been hard for what seemed like hours.

I struggled with the need to ejaculate, I needed to cum desperately. It was like a surge tide pushing against a flimsy wooden sea wall. It seemed I was permanently on the verge of cumming these days. They controlled my penis. I was desperate to touch myself and let the flood burst out in a beautiful release. It was not about to happen any time soon.

We sat in silence for ten minutes, Imogen was not one for small talk. She didn't like me either.

"The next exercise begins now, girl," Imogen suddenly announced.

Exercise, my least favourite activity. I slumped in despair. I couldn't physically do anything more, every muscle in my legs hurt from their odd raised position in the heels. I had blisters on both my big toes.

"Don't worry, girl, it's speaking exercises. Your voice is too masculine so we need to raise the tone to a pitch that's more feminine." She let her words sink in.

I was tired and I didn't want to play any more of her games. I didn't want her messing around with my voice for no reason. I'd be out in six weeks so what was the point? Imogen wasn't bothered by my surly expression.

"Say after me, girl. I want to be a sissy girl and I want to wear short pretty dresses."

I sighed, too loudly.

Imogen came at me with her paddle raised. She pushed me off the chair and sat down on it herself. I froze, not knowing what was going to happen. The answer came as she pulled me over her knee by an ear. She pulled up my dress. Her paddle came down hard with a slap that echoed around the ground floor, then another and another. Maja scurried out from a door to see what was going on. She stopped, looked, grunted and went back to the kitchen.

Ten slaps stung against my buttocks before Imogen pushed me away. I fell on the floor, my skirt around my waist and legs apart like a dog submitting to the leader of the pack.

Imogen slid down onto the floor and knelt in front of me. "Stay as you are, girl."

I wanted to cover up, I wanted to run, I wanted to scream at her. Instead, I bit my tongue and replied, "Yes Madam Imogen." I couldn't blink such was my embarrassment and shame at my exposure.

She leant forward and put two fingers on the head of my erection. A fizz of electricity exploded on the head of my penis around where her fingertips were now touching. A small drop of pre-cum oozed out of the tip, like an old man drooling over a young girl. I wanted to cum so badly, I closed my eyes as the pressure built. Just the feel of her fingers was causing my desperation to reach a boiling point.

Imogen slid my foreskin back fully. Her finger lingered on the swollen gland and rolled-up skin. I arched my back as I felt the build-up. I waited for her to slide her fingers back up my red bulbous end, slowly, softly. Then down again, I hoped. My juices would reach that boiling point in the depth of my balls and prostate, like a bubbling liquid in a witch's cauldron about to overflow. Her fingers hovered a moment more, a light touch of a butterfly that fluttered away and all I sensed was a brush of air.

I opened my eyes and Imogen was glaring at me without blinking.

"I need to cum, Madam Imogen, please."

My desperate whisper was met with a flick of her fingernail on the exposed head of my straining erection. A small ringing sound against the Prince Albert ring. She looked at it and then at me and flicked it again. She was never going to masturbate me, she had something else in mind.

"We're starting your elocution lessons and any silliness from you where you don't speak correctly, then I will slap your little clitty. And you won't want that on your little sensitive exposed girly bits, will you?"

"No, Madam, I won't," I croaked. An aching flowed down my erection and into my tight balls where the cauldron of retrained semen continued to bubble like a hot potion.

Imogen towered over my wide-open legs and raging erection. Maja strolled into the room with a bottle of water. Her hard expression softened in surprise for a tiny instant as she saw my position sitting back, legs wide apart. She resumed her aggressive look, like that of a petulant child. She placed the water on the floor next to Imogen with two glasses and walked out again not looking back.

"I've trained many sissies to speak like little girls and I will succeed with you too, girl, so there's no point trying to resist me." She gave a rare smile. "In fact," she said, "let's go straight to the lisp. Say after me, girl, in a sweet high girly voice, I want to be a *thithy* and I want wear *pwitty dwesses* and skirts for *Mith-twith*."

I looked at her horrified for several moments. Her riding crop hovered over my erection. I repeated her words with a dry throat, "I want to be a *thithy* and I want to wear *pwitty dwesses* and skirts for *Mith-twith*."

I sounded like a high-pitched rock singer with laryngitis. Whack, Imogen's crop slapped against my penis head and I doubled up. She then poured some water and gave it to me. I guzzled it down.

"You will say that again, girl, but much higher in tone and softer in manner."

I put the drained glass down. Drained like me. "I want to be a *thithy* and wear *pwitty dwesses* and skirts for *Mith-twith*."

I said it.

Whack, her crop slapped against my erection. Then again. "You sound like a cartoon character, you stupid girl. Copy my tone." Imogen said the words carefully and I tried again. Another slap and she gave three flicks with her fingernails against the slit at the top of my erection.

"You're useless, girl. If you want to be a sissy you will need to talk like one. Now repeat with me this time."

I stopped myself telling her I didn't want to be a girl by holding my mouth tight.

We continued repeating the same line over and over. The slaps and flicks reduced as I managed to come closer to the tone and delivery she wanted. Eventually, she got up and told me I could go to my room and relax. She told me I had done OK in the end but there was a long way to go.

"Even sissy girls have to relax," she said, adding, "Maja has put several things in your room to help you."

I knew that would not help me one little bit.

9 Sissy

I went to my room. Maja had indeed left several items scattered around for me. My heart sank as I saw there were girls' magazines about makeup, relationships and clothes spread all over my bed. There were a couple of paperbacks about true romance with titles such as *'She Loved the Boy Next Door'* and *'A Pretty Girl's Love'*. I saw a jewellery-making kit, full of plastic beads and coloured string.

On the side unit by the bed, a large bunch of different types of flowers was laid out, a glass vase and a book on flower arranging beside them. On the other unit was a large book with a photo of cakes on the front sleeve and a large red title exclaiming *Cake Decorating for Girls*.

I was trying hard to pretend to accept my temporary feminisation but I didn't want to read this rubbish. There's a limit. I spotted one magazine under the pile. I extracted it and looked at it in disbelief. It was full of naked photos of young men, many with huge erections. I threw it across the room.

My entire body slumped and I sauntered to the window. I gazed out to the front garden, through the old apple trees and to the road beyond. The window was ajar and the smell of cut grass and jasmine from the terracotta pot below wafted in on a soft breeze. It rustled against my long hair. I wanted fresh air and a walk in the late afternoon summer sun. The back garden would be more secluded.

I went down the stairs and passed into the kitchen where a silent aggressive Maja glared at me. I opened the back door and went outside into the warm sunlight. A flagstone patio area led to a lower lawn area behind a retaining brick wall. A wooden patio table and chairs stood at one side of the patio area. The garden was beautiful and I relaxed.

It would help me to forget my incarceration for a few brief carefree moments.

It was obvious that Melissa had a gardener; the garden was surrounded by trees and high neat hedges and totally secluded. I felt comfortable with the idea that I was free to wander without being seen by the neighbours despite wearing a short white summer mini-dress and high-heeled shoes. Not to speak of my hairstyle and makeup.

I stepped down onto the grass and my thin heels sank a half inch into the lush turf. The garden was around 100 feet long and I strolled to the end, enjoying the fresh air and clearing my head. At the end, two willows with drooping branches that kissed the ground. The soil was harder here as it was more open to the sun.

A six-foot high wooden fence ran along the back of the garden with small ground bushes and flowers growing up against it. A smell of protective paint mingled with the smell of blossom. There was another garden beyond the fence. I walked up to the barrier and the light breeze played with the hem of my dress. It rubbed against my smooth legs and penis. The breeze lifted the dress above my near-constant erection. There was no one here and the freedom of the warm open air was intoxicating so I ignored it and let my dress blow.

I glanced over the fence and shook my head back to let my hair flow around my face and neck. That was a mistake. Lying in the garden on a sun lounger facing me was a young man in shorts and a bare chest. Bronzed and slim, his eyes were hidden behind large sunglasses. He sat up and called out. "Hello."

I pulled my head back and bent back down. Panic. At least he hadn't seen my dress blowing up. He called out again, "Hello?". I remained crouched down behind the fence, why had I risked being seen? I'd got carried away with being free from Imogen. I had let my guard down.

"Hello, pretty lady, you're a shy one."

I jerked my head up and his grinning sunglasses-covered face was peering down at me over the fence.

"I haven't seen you before. I would definitely have noticed *you*."

Oh no, he was flirting with me. I put my head down and then back up again. He was still there, a head and two sets of fingers on the top of the fence. Now closer up, I could see the lines in his angular face. He had kept himself well but the grey in his hair and the wrinkles told me he was closer to my own age; early forties. This was not good.

"Nice to meet you.," I said "I have to get back in the house, sorry. In a rush. Can't talk." I tried my best high-pitched girly voice, just as Imogen had been teaching me. Her training session had become more useful more quickly than I'd expected.

"I'm Nick, I live here. What's your name?"

"Jos..., Joanne." I concentrated on using my best girl voice. I focussed on how Imogen had taught me to speak like a girl. Nick remained at the fence. He wasn't going away.

"That's a pretty dress, Joanne. Do you live here now?"

"For the summer only. I'm staying here with...." What should I call them? "I'm staying with Mistr..., with Melissa." I had to concentrate to not make a mistake.

"Great, maybe we can see a bit more of each other when you have more time. I'll keep a look out for you and we can have a longer chat next time. There aren't so many pretty girls around here, Joanne. Only that miserable Maja. She's so unfriendly and Melissa but she's out at work a lot."

"Sorry, Nick, I have to get back in." I stood and backed away as Nick ogled me. *Ogled me?* I hated the look of desire on his face, luckily I couldn't see his eyes which I imagined sparkled with lust. I shivered at the prospect and moved back, step by step. A gust came through the violet-blossomed tree to my left and swept against my dress, catching it like the sails on a galleon. My hands flew to my dress, I had no panties on. The dress waved against my hands but I held it down. Just. Nick watched and grinned. That was too close. I could never risk that again.

"I hope I can see more of you soon, Joanne." His innuendo fired around my brain like a pinball. "A pretty name for a pretty girl."

I brushed the dress down as the gust dropped and ran back towards the house. I stumbled in my heels and fell to my knees. I picked myself up and staggered back and into the kitchen.

"So, you meet Nick."

Maja's impassive face met mine as I stumbled in. I turned back to see Nick still at the end of the garden. He waved at me

"He divorce and live alone. He need woman. He too much old for me but I say he perfect for you, Joanne." Maja left the implication hanging despite her garbled grammar.

I thought I saw the beginnings of a smile on her lips. I shuddered at the thought of Nick finding me attractive. If I wanted to go out again, I'd now have to stay close to the back of the house and not venture down to the end of the garden again. That way I wouldn't meet Nick again. Or so I thought.

10 Melissa's story

Melissa didn't need to travel on public transport. She could afford a big car and a chauffeur. But she enjoyed taking the train to work and home. The train journey gave her time to think and unwind. Much better than the stress of fighting the gridlocked city traffic and much quicker.

The train was busy but there was always a seat by the time she left work, a long time after rush hour finished. Melissa glanced at her reflection in the window opposite as they entered a tunnel, leaving the light of the station behind them. She pouted her lips and fluffed her hair with a hand. Thirty-eight and looking good. *You get nothing without intense effort.* That was her mantra and the hours in the gym and beauty parlours had paid off handsomely she thought to herself.

She turned her head to one side and then the other admiringly. A young man in a cheap black suit and pointed brown shoes was staring at her but looked away from her withering stare. She enjoyed the attention even if she would never have anything to do with someone dressed like a cheap estate agent. Young was good, not cheap. She understood his lust for her. She was looking damn good in a sharp expensive business suit, pencil skirt to her knees and killer heels. Business clothes were great but it was nice to put on something sexier once she got home.

She was surprised to feel an approaching sense of excitement as her stop got closer. Closer to see how her transformation of that useless loser Joseph was progressing. He wasn't the first feminisation she'd overseen but he was the most personal. His wife Julie was her best friend from school. And she'd never liked him.

The loser still thought that once he had shown sufficient remorse and humiliation she would return him to Julie and he could revert to being a male again. Melissa was convinced he would never change his ways so she didn't plan on ever letting him go back to masculinity. She knew it was all an act; he was going along with her changes with little fuss until he thought she would get bored. It was easy to see through him.

She had experienced that type of man before. Her own father. A taker and a chancer who had systematically taken advantage of her dear mother for years. He'd never held down a regular job, drinking and going with other women. Just like Joseph. When she first met Joseph, she knew he was cut from the same cloth as her father. She'd tried to convince Julie not to marry him but Julie had fallen for his boyish charm and his promises to change his ways.

Now Julie had passed Joseph to her to deal with and there was only one solution. He was to become a submissive sissy girl. There would be no going back for Joseph despite what he thought. He would become Joanne and he would eventually accept it. It was about getting him to the point where he didn't want to go back to being a man. If not, when he couldn't go back. Then he would be cured. There was no other solution for men like him.

She knew she would face resistance from Julie. Julie was soft and spoilt. Her parents were wealthy and her mother was overbearing. At least Julie's father Charles worked hard. He was under her mother Verity's firm control. That was good and how it should be. Without that firm female control, men will always stray and be lazy. They were like children. It was probably the only reason Charles behaved. It was the only way for men. Melissa would have gone further with Julie's father and put him in a little dress and high heels. It wasn't her problem though, it was Julie's mother's. She had Joseph to play with.

Once home she would effect the cool image she had so carefully manufactured. It wouldn't do for anyone to see the real Melissa. The working-class kid made good. Exceptionally good. Who would have thought that the tall confident Melissa Stone in designer wear used to be skinny Mary Cullen wearing charity shop cast-offs? Changing her name was necessary, she needed something strong to reflect her adopted façade. She needed to be reborn as someone else. Mary Cullen was a nice pretty name but she needed to project power and privilege. She needed a strong middle-class name and a change in her back story. Melissa had googled middle-class names and chose the name Melissa. Stone as a surname spoke for itself.

The train pulled into the next station and the passengers getting off were smart, professional and wealthy. Like her. They hadn't had to work as hard as her to get to where she was today, they would have had rich parents to smooth their way. A place at university then a guaranteed position at daddy's firm or the friend of daddy's firm. They didn't need a scholarship, the poor girl in the class. They didn't work nights stacking supermarket shelves to pay their way.

She had something they didn't have though. They didn't have their own bad boy to mould into something better for the world. She couldn't get revenge on her father, he had died a few years ago. Cirrhosis of the liver, no more than he deserved. But she did have Joseph. He would do.

Melissa's mother had died some years after her father, probably from exhaustion. She had tried to help but her mother was too proud. Too working class. Her reflection in the opposite window disappeared as the low evening sun glared in. She glanced over to the estate agent whose head spun away; caught out again.

The train came to a halt at her stop. She marched off the train and up the stairs and through the ticket barriers to the high street. A passing electric-powered bus whooshed by, hot air following in its wake and blowing Melissa's hair across her face. Her hair could take the tussled look, it would look even more alluring.

As she tramped up the hill to her home from the high street, the excitement grew. She strode forward like an officer leading a foot patrol back to the home lines. Imogen, her personal fitness instructor and sometime female domination associate at the club, would have Joseph slash Joanne waiting for inspection. Imogen had been a good find. Loyal and a born soldier. A former army captain who had left the forces and, like many from the army, used her knowledge and experience of fitness to make a career for herself. Imogen also had an interesting sideline in her spare time working from a dungeon she rented. Femdom. Weak men paid her to humiliate them. A good woman.

Mandy was very different, a girly girl who for some reason loved pink and frills. This disguised a keen business brain and Mandy was one of her dearest friends. Melissa thought Mandy might be a good look to model Joseph on. She had lots of ideas for Joseph and the blonde bimbo look was just one. Nevertheless, Melissa liked Mandy as she reminded her of herself many years ago. Mandy's accent and background were not that different from what hers used to be. They even came from the same poor borough. Mandy had chosen a different route and was one of the best in her field. That was why Mandy was now her personal beautician and was more than happy to offer her services feminising the males Melissa brought to her.

Melissa walked off the high street and headed towards her home at a steady strut. It didn't matter to her that her father was out of reach now. If there was an afterlife, she imagined he was somewhere hot and uncomfortable. She had Joseph to work out her frustration on. He would improve, he already had. There was so much more to do and that was exciting. Seeing him in short dresses, long feminine hair and acting submissive was sublime. He thought it was all a game. A game to punish him. It was so much more than that.

Joseph was pretending to go along with her demands. She knew that. Soon the point would come when he would be more girl than boy and only then would she be satisfied. She didn't know what that point was yet. She hoped he would start to enjoy the clothing and the lifestyle and one day she was sure he would. She had already seen the signs. She would go as far as necessary to get him to womanhood and to do whatever it took. To the point when Joseph became Joanne.

11 The Schoolgirl Look

Melissa arrived home just after 8.30. I'd heard her come in while I was laying on the bed dozing. Imogen had fixed my cock cage on before I'd gone to my room and I was fiddling with it to make it more comfortable, trying to pull my balls through the ring which pinched. Imogen was not careful when she locked it on me.

I heard Imogen and Melissa chatting in the hall as soon as she got in but I couldn't make out what they were saying. Five minutes later, Imogen appeared. She had changed from earlier into tight black leather trousers and knee-high boots. I'd not yet seen her in a skirt or dress. Without speaking, she went to my wardrobe and began rifling through the dresses hanging there. All I wanted was to lie there feeling sorry for myself.

I heard her say, "Ah." She'd found what she wanted.

She flung the dress across my legs and she told me to change for dinner and inspection. I looked in horror and what she had chosen. It was a pink and white checked gingham dress with a white collar. A schoolgirl's uniform dress. I'd not noticed it in the wardrobe although I hadn't spent any time going through my dresses if I'm honest. I didn't want to think about what I was being forced to wear.

I looked in abject horror at the small pink and white squares that covered the dress. The bright white high collar was done up with three white buttons from the top of the chest to the neck. A box-pleated skirt made me feel faint at the prospect of something so feminine and girly. The sleeves were short with a small puffy shoulder detail.

I sat up, this was the worst dress I could ever have thought of having to wear. It was humiliating enough to have to wear a short white summer dress, but a schoolgirl's dress was worse.

"It's a dress for schoolgirls, Ma'am," I complained. "I can't wear this."

"It is indeed a schoolgirl's uniform dress, girl. Put it on and let's go and show Melissa how well you've done today. You're already looking much more feminine after just one day."

The sun outside was low in the sky and flowed into my room through the wide leaves of the apple tree giving a dappled effect to the evening light. A large magpie was making a harsh repetitive call in the branches. I was low on energy and I would have preferred to sleep. I mused that it was the lack of carbs.

I pulled myself up with a deep lethargy as Imogen folded her arms impatiently. I removed my white summer dress and pulled on the schoolgirl dress. I smoothed down my thick long hair and rubbed my neck where the high collar touched it. I pulled my feet into white ankle-high socks that Imogen had passed me and then into the dreaded high-heeled shoes. My calves ached as soon as I stood.

Imogen grinned. She didn't smile much and this outfit amused her. She stood behind me and pushed her hands against my arms and manoeuvred me towards the mirror. From the neck down I was a schoolgirl. My 45-year-old vaguely masculine face did not fit the rest of the image despite my false eyelashes and makeup.

My bare hairless legs finished in bright white ankle socks. They had a tiny pink frill around the top. The dress was longer than the white one so that was a blessing of sorts. It sat about midway between my crotch and my knee. Imogen's beaming face reflected from over my right shoulder. I wanted to know why she enjoyed humiliating me, someone she hardly knew. I didn't dare to ask her and it probably didn't matter. She was going to do it whatever her reasons. Maybe she had man issues, Melissa certainly did.

Imogen tapped my bottom with her crop which indicated it was time to go downstairs for my inspection by Melissa. My reflection in the mirror was that of a girl and not the man I should be. Melissa would be pleased with my progress, I was certain of that. I was not pleased but that didn't matter. Besides, once I'd convinced Melissa I was a reformed character and I'd been punished enough, I could go back to Julie and things could return to normal. I would have to be far more careful about the girls I met and I'd have to reduce my alcohol intake. I'd even make sure I held onto a job. This current period would then be just a bad memory.

That was still six weeks away at the earliest and my head went down and my spirits seeped away. Six weeks. I had to be strong. Imogen pulled at the hair on one side of my head. She twisted one hand and put an elastic tie in and made a long ponytail above one ear. Another twisting motion and the other side became a ponytail too.

I put my hands to my face and I covered my eyes in horror. She tied something on both sides and I peeked through my fingers. She had put two large pink ribbons on either side to increase the schoolgirl look. Side ponytails! She spun me around and brushed my fringe to my eyes and then turned me back to look at myself in the mirror again. It was the most humiliating look I'd been given so far and I'd had a few. I stared in the mirror, not understanding how it had come to this. Me, a, 'Jack the lad' now reduced to being dressed up like a schoolgirl.

Imogen beckoned me to follow her downstairs with a slow movement of her forefinger, as if I were a naughty schoolboy. Or should I say, schoolgirl? I trudged towards her and down the stairs and towards the dining room, barely lifting my feet. The white door of the living room was ajar and I heard Melissa chatting with Mandy. I heard the sound of Maja's distinctive rapid footsteps clipping around.

Imogen pushed me through first and the room went silent. Maja descended into a fit of giggles. Imogen pushed me closer to the sofa where Melissa and Mandy were sitting, each with a china cup of tea in their hands, sitting at the table. I stopped before Melissa and her eyes widened like bright porcelain dinner plates. A slow grin formed across her lips. I remembered to curtsey which caused a wider grin. She motioned for me to twirl around. Mandy's resolve broke at this point and she gave out a high-pitched laugh, like a machine gun. Rat-tat-a-tat. She snorted through her nose as she lost control of her laughter.

Melissa watched me turn around holding the hem of my dress. "Imogen and Mandy, you've done a fantastic job here. Well done. I can't believe what you've achieved in one day."

I stopped after the full 360 degrees and faced Melissa. She indicated that I lift my dress to reveal my cock cage holding in a struggling erection. The tip pressed hard against the end of the device. Melissa looked concerned and screwed her forehead.

"Imogen, why don't we let her out of that thing for dinner? She won't touch herself with us here, I'm sure it's safe."

Imogen unlocked the padlock and my penis fell out with a grateful surge which only made Mandy let out a machine-gun rattle of a laugh once again. Imogen clipped on the cat bell. Melissa hadn't told me to drop my dress hem yet so I continued to stand there holding it up while they looked at my erection. Melissa took the head between two fingers and squeezed and then pulled. I wasn't sure why but I supposed she was showing she could do as she pleased. Which she could.

"It's such as pathetic little thing." Melissa's eyes looked up at me. Her face was almost on my erection. "How did any woman ever get any satisfaction from this? Poor Julie, no wonder she was never that happy."

I wondered if Mandy was going to have an injury such was the extent of her laughing. She was red in the face. "A schoolgirl," she said through giggles. "Genius."

Melissa changed the subject. "Tomorrow Mandy will start a course of electrolysis on the hair around your little clitty and your legs and body. Schoolgirls can't have hair."

Mandy stared intently at my penis. It was shaved smooth with a perfect female triangle of trimmed pubic hair above it. "I won't have time to do her whole body with electrolysis tomorrow so maybe I'll start around here?" Mandy's long fingernail traced my pubic triangle.

I didn't like the idea of waxing and I was unsure what she meant by electrolysis. I had a vague idea that electrolysis was a permanent hair removal technique. I needed to ask Mandy if that was true. If this was all a humiliation game because of my bad behaviour and permanence wasn't part of the deal. If there was a deal.

"Miss Mandy, may I ask a question?" I knew I had to be extremely polite so that my question would be answered and I didn't incur any punishment. Nonetheless, Melissa scowled at me and Imogen's body tightened. I had to be careful. I wanted to avoid any confrontation that meant my future return to masculinity would be jeopardised.

Mandy was less aggressive and looked at me, the final jerks of her giggles now subsiding. Although she had a breezy friendly personality, she still enjoyed the respect I had to give her. "Yes, Joanne, go ahead," she said.

"I thought that electrolysis was a permanent hair removal technique. My feminisation is only temporary."

Mandy hesitated then her head swung to look at Melissa for an answer. That didn't look promising. Melissa's scowl softened. I dropped my dress front back over my erection thinking that the atmosphere had lightened. Melissa's face instantly reverted to the scowl. "Did I say you could cover your little schoolgirl clitty, Joanne?"

I yanked my dress hem back up to my stomach and my erection was back on show. Whack, Imogen's riding crop came down on the exposed head of my erection and I doubled over in shock as the cat's bell tinkled.

She lifted my head with a forefinger. I stood tall again, both hands on my dress, holding it up to my stomach. Melissa returned a fingernail to my pubic area and traced out the size of the shape of the pubic triangle she wanted Mandy to make tomorrow. I squeezed my eyes tightly as the soft feel of her nails trailed around the base of my penis. Although I wanted to cum badly, her fingernail wasn't providing enough sensation to stimulate the orgasm.

She lifted my penis with her fingernail and I opened one eye as she poked my balls and explained to Mandy that my 'pussy area' was to be completely clean of any hair. Except for the little girl's pubic triangle, of course.

Maja burst back into the room, the greasy smell of hot chicken coming with her. She placed a tray of food on the dining table. She left and returned twice more with vegetables and potatoes in serving bowls and placed them on the table for dinner. She came back one last time with a spoon and the chrome dog's bowl with my food in and put it on the floor next to Melissa's feet. I had to sit on the floor again. The bowl contained my meal of salad leaves and other light food, all without dressing.

Mandy, Imogen and Melissa sat around the table and I sat on the floor next to Melissa's feet. No one had answered my question about whether electrolysis was permanent or not.

12 Depilation

My naked body stung. Mandy had spent the morning waxing almost every part of me. She kept up a constant monologue about everything from TV soaps to handbags.

I was pretending to read one of several magazines that Imogen had given me; *Women's Allure*. It was about makeup and other beauty tips. How to find the best moisturiser, adding colour to your face, the ten best eye shadows and so on. They were pushing female psychology on me. Everything they did was about femininity. It could have been worse, it could have been that magazine with naked men again.

At least Mandy was kind although being told I had sexy feminine legs was not what I had wanted to hear. She meant well, I suppose. She thought I wanted to be a girl. Or she pretended to think that, I wasn't sure.

I relaxed when I was with her as she didn't seem to hate me like Imogen and Melissa did. Or Maja with her passive contempt, especially when she was washing my penis and balls as I held my hands in the air. Mandy worked away, chatting and smiling. She even made me a cup of coffee. She told me I had been a, *"Brave girl"*, after she'd finished with the waxing, a marathon three-hour session. She added that she usually did this in smaller stages spread over days but Melissa wanted me depilated as quickly as possible.

I lay back in the chair feeling uncomfortably exposed. I was completely naked; Mandy had insisted so she could get on with her work unhindered. My almost permanent erection was in my line of sight, the foreskin completely retracted and the ring and bells mocking me. My pink shellac toenails glistened under the halogen lamps directed at my body. Mandy sat back, chatting and chewing gum speaking about nothing in particular. I wasn't sure if she was talking to me or herself.

Maja came in and delivered lunch. I had a bowl of tomato, lettuce and cucumber. She turned back to glance at me as she left, a sneer escaping from her face and her eyes dropped to my erection. Mandy had chicken too but I was still on Imogen's diet.

Mandy told me she was going to start the electrolysis after we had eaten. I didn't feel hungry at hearing that which was just as well as my salad looked boring, especially as it didn't have any dressing. Imogen wanted to keep my calorie intake low. Mandy told me that the electrolysis would take several days to complete in daily sessions.

I wanted to know if it was a permanent hair removal. "My body hair will grow back, won't it?"

She giggled nervously before answering. "Do you think Melissa would do anything that left you permanently feminine?"

That was an enigmatic answer. I hoped even Melissa wouldn't go that far.

Mandy looked embarrassed. "Joanne, darling, if you understand how Melissa thinks and acts particularly regarding males, you'd know the answer to your question."

This was an enigmatic answer too. At times, her bubbly girly manner became something else. Something deeper. I saw that her style and constant chatting were a front. However, her answer left me believing the answer was no but with a pang of doubt. This was probably part of Melissa's strategy – to make me uncomfortable. She had achieved this, that much was certain.

Mandy finished her food and wheeled her chair over to where I was laying back on the dentist-type chair. My feet were on the end of the foot supports. The sensation of being at a dentist increased as she pulled over a spotlight above my head. Instead of my teeth, she shone it on my genitals. Her peroxide blonde hair fell across my erection like a curtain being drawn on my masculinity. She pulled my legs apart as wide as they would go and chuckled to herself.

She held a pen-like device in her left hand that she moved past her curtain of hair to my crotch region. She pressed it to the shaft of my erect penis. I jumped a little at a slight stinging sensation. For the next thirty minutes, she worked her way down my penis and around my balls. It wasn't a bad feeling and, as she moved, her long hair trailed around my stomach and occasionally across my penis and balls.

This did nothing to help my desperation to ejaculate and was an accidental but erotic tease. As she worked, she held my erection lightly between two latex-gloved fingers. She manoeuvring around to get to the hair follicles on and around my genitals. I closed my eyes to enjoy the focus on my penis, her fingers and the small stings from the electrolysis pen were not unpleasant.

Maja would also touch my penis and balls when she washed me but she was rough and sneering with a look of disgust. Mandy was gentler and caring although in the context of me being just another customer. Mandy moved onto my pubic area. It was neat and triangular, but she worked at the edges, her pen steady and methodical as she formed a perfect small triangle. She had made it smaller than I had. Another thirty minutes passed as I basked in the sensation of her hair tickling my bare denuded balls.

The door to the parlour banged and I opened my eyes to see Imogen strut in. Today, more than ever, she looked like the model from a recruitment poster for the army. She was dressed in a dark khaki vest and her muscled arms were defined, strong and firm. The vest hugged her breasts and the outline of a sports bra peeked out. She wore military-style baggy combat trousers with side pockets that hung from her wide hips. The trousers were tucked into knee-high riding boots.

Mandy shot her a glance. "Almost done, *Imy*."
"No rush, *Mands*."

Each of the two women used familiar names for each other showing how comfortable they were with each other.

Mandy finished a few minutes later. Imogen bent over to inspect her work around my penis and pubic hair and grunted her approval. She motioned for me to get up. "Get dressed, girl."

Imogen always selected my clothing and she gave me a tight white blouse to put on and a skin-tight black micro pencil skirt. I slipped them on. My erect penis poked below the hem, it was so short. I slipped on my bra and pushed in the breast forms. I pulled on my blouse. Imogen was holding a white plastic bag.

"Girl," said Imogen. "Now your legs are smooth and hair-free, it's time you wore stockings." She pulled out a cardboard packet and then a black suspender belt which she passed to me. I slumped at the prospect of this latest humiliation. I sat on the 'dentist chair' and ran my hands down my legs. They were a different level of smoothness than from shaving. There was a nice sensation to them and, for a moment, I lost myself in the feelings.

A cough from Imogen brought me around. Mandy giggled. They had both been watching me and my face reddened. What had I been thinking? I'd got carried away with the feeling of my smooth feminised legs. I vowed to get myself out of this mindset.

As I did up the suspender belt, I knew that the constant increase on feminisation was having an effect on me. I had been going along with the punishment but for the first time, I'd forgotten that it was a punishment. I'd enjoyed Mandy's depilation of my body and then the feel of my smooth feminine skin. I shook my head, annoyed at my stupid thoughts.

Imogen ripped open the cardboard packet and handed me a pair of fine black stockings. I took them and allowed them to fall from my hand. They had a laced pattern like a fishing net. My erection strained, I hadn't thought it possible to be any stronger. The sight of the stockings brought out such a straining hard-on that I thought for a moment my skin would snap. I pulled the first stocking over my feet and up my leg. Imogen clipped it in place to the suspender belt. I pulled the other stocking up and Imogen clipped it in place too.

My skirt was more like a handkerchief of material. It was cotton with a sheer black lining. I stood and Imogen passed me some shoes. They were a new pair and I stifled a cry of horror. They were glossy black patent shoes with a single thin strap that would fit around my leg above the ankle. They had super thin heels that must have been at least six inches high.

"Ma'am. I won't be able to walk in these. I struggle in the four-inch heels."

Imogen harrumphed then replied. "The four-inchers were just for starters. This is what you'll be practising walking in today, and for the next few weeks."

I was aghast as I took them and put them on each foot. They slid on and I stood up, tottering unsteadily. I was, in effect, walking on tip-toes. The rest of my foot was upright at right angles. I tried walking to the stairs. It was like walking on stilts. I felt like a fairground attraction for the amusement of these ladies.

Imogen helped me up the stairs to the living area, holding my arm like a care worker helping an old infirm woman. The effect of my erection and going up the stairs had reduced my skirt to a belt and it bunched around my stomach. I hated the sound of that cat's bell every time I made a movement.

We went up and into the living room with Imogen holding my arm to steady me. Imogen sat and made me walk up and down in the shoes. More walking training. I constantly pulled my skirt down over my erection, but one step later, it would ride up again. Up and down I went for two hours. My calved hurt, crying out for rest. Eventually, I was able to find a method that allowed me to walk steadily. I saw the purpose of the tight skirt. If I took very small steps, it didn't ride up so easily. It made me take smaller steps as I walked up and down, up and down.

Imogen nodded and said, "Good girl," a few times. She was content with my progress. "Take a five-minute break, girl, then you'll practise sitting like a sissy."

I sat on a wooden chair. Imogen came over to me and crossed my legs for me. "I want you to sit like a girl. Always cross your legs and keep them close together. Girls who wear short skirts, like you will always do, need to be more demure. You don't want to show your goods to the boys, or do you?"

She was making me annoyed. She made me stand, sit, cross my legs. Stand, sit then cross my legs. This went on for the next hour. My leg muscles were crying out for relief and my toes were crushed against the front of my shoes. Imogen announced after the hour that this was enough for today and then guided me up to my bedroom. I noticed that as I progressed deeper into feminisation, Imogen treated me better. She hadn't spanked me all day. Instead, she had held my arm to help me navigate the stairs in my new six-inch high shoes back to my bedroom. I hoped that this was all for the day and there would be no more surprises.

I was to be disappointed. Very disappointed.

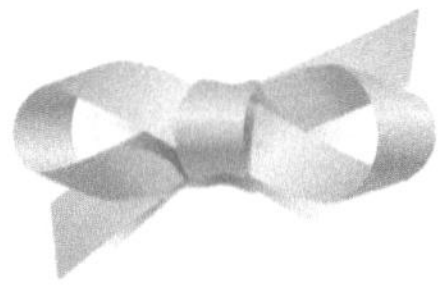

13 Maid to measure

I stood by my bed as Imogen fixed on my chastity cage and then pointed to the women's magazines. "Read the nice girly magazines, sissy, and relax."

She picked up the one with naked young men and opened it to a full-page photo of a man with muscles and an enormous penis hanging low and loose. I turned away, feeling a little sick at the sight of that.

"Enjoy looking at sexy boys, sissy girl." her eyes sparkled. "Imagine that cock in your sissy mouth."

She marched out of my room and I saw that the door had been removed. I wondered when that had happened, it must have been when I was in the basement beauty parlour. I couldn't even shut myself away in private any more.

I sat on the bed and threw the magazine of naked men across the bed. I picked up one of the other magazines, *Fashion for Girls*. I had nothing else to do so I flicked through it, better than seeing photos of men with huge cocks and giant balls.

I lay back on the bed and started to read. I'd been wearing female clothing for a couple of weeks and I would have to do so for some weeks to come. I guessed it might be useful to see what options there were and to find out more. I'd also need to keep my hair and makeup done well.

I became absorbed in the articles, learning about the latest dresses and scarves, skirts and blouses and the latest colour schemes and accessories. The early evening summer sun filtered through the windows and the dust particles in the air danced in the heat.

"Well, well, reading girly magazines. What a good sissy. Excellent work, *Imy*." I hadn't heard Melissa and Imogen at the entrance to my room.

Melissa stood tall and proud, legs apart like a gunslinger from the American Wild West. Except she was dressed as a modern businesswoman in a knee-length fitted skirt and matching jacket. A chill ran through me despite the early evening humidity.

'Clap clap' came from Imogen's hands. I didn't know what she wanted at first. Then I remembered and jumped up to curtsey each of them in turn, my tight micro skirt riding up showing my cage and exposing the suspender belt that held up my patterned stockings.

Imogen made for my wardrobe and slid the dresses along the pole as she searched for something specific. I was being made to constantly change into ever more humiliating outfits. She lifted a pink dress off the hanger and held it out to me. It was a pink Victorian-style maid's outfit which flared out from the waist with stiff white frilly petticoats. I took it with despair. Every time I thought it could get no worse but it got worse.

"Put it on, Joanne," said Melissa. "We need to push on with your training and there's so much to do. And it's time you began working for me to pay your keep. You're going to be helping Maja around the house. Cleaning, washing, ironing and so on. Whatever she tells you to do."

"No!" I screamed. I couldn't help myself, it had slipped out without a thought. My old self was still bubbling below the new surface and burst out. I threw the dress down and stamped a high-heeled foot. My inner feelings had erupted, like a volcano bursting through a thin membrane. I'd managed to keep a lid on my emotions even if it meant wearing humiliating clothing, being exposed and wearing female hairstyles. All this had meant me switching off and waiting until Melissa had determined I was 'ready'. Working for Maja though, this was a step too far.

Melissa maintained her cool and folded her arms. "This isn't a negotiation, Joanne sissy. And you will never speak like that to any woman." She turned to Imogen. "Imy, you know what to do."

Imogen pulled me up by my hair and swung me around. She pushed the back of my neck down so that my forehead was pushed into my bed mattress. My skirt scrunched up to my waist and my bare bum faced her. My caged penis and loose balls swung between my legs.

Whack, whack, whack. Her paddle rained down spanks against my bare buttocks. The whacks continued until raw heat glowed off the sore skin. She finished and pulled me up.

"Remove your clothing now, sissy, and put the maid's dress on. Keep your stockings and shoes on," Imogen ordered.

So much for not being spanked today. I put a hand on my buttocks. They were burning hot. I took off my pencil skirt and blouse and put the maid's dress on. At least it covered my erection which continued to be strong and resistant to everything they did. Or was it because of what they did to me?

Imogen put a firm hand on my arm and pulled me to the full-length mirror. She always made me look at myself in the mirror after every change. I was in a bright pastel-pink-flared housemaid's dress. The puffy sleeves came partway down each of my skinny arms. A small brilliant white apron was tied around my waist. I still had the fish-net stockings and six-inch heels on and I knew not to point out the difficulty I would have in working in them.

I struggled down to the kitchen in my super-high heels. My toe joints were sore as all my weight fell on them in these horrid yet oddly exciting shoes. In the kitchen, Maja was wiping down the oven and stopped when we all entered. The smell of disinfectant and lemon from her cleaning products stung my nose. Imogen touched my shoulders to remind me to curtsey to all women, even Maja. I was thankful the dress was longer than the pencil skirt I had been wearing during the day.

"We'll leave you girls together," Melissa said and left with Imogen.

Maja scowled and I thought I heard a growl. She didn't like me and I guessed I'd now given her extra work. She wiggled a finger at me indicating that I follow her. I staggered into the utility area next to the kitchen. A pile of damp clothing was piled up in a large plastic clothes basket.

"Put *zeess* on clothes line in garden. *Zey* need dry," she said, struggling to pronounce the 'th' sounds.

"It's a little late in the day, Miss Maja," I said remembering to address her correctly despite my logical brain trying to prevent me.

'Slap,' a hand stung my face. "Do not *qvestion* me, sissy girl. Melissa say you do *ev'rysing* I tell you."

I looked out to the garden. The sun was low but it was still light and warm. I glanced at the 6ft fence and decided it was too high for anyone to see me. Nick specifically. The rotary line was partway up the garden. I had no choice so I lifted the clothes basket and stumbled out to the garden. I walked over the stone patio and onto the garden. A stepping-stone path to the clothesline allowed me to avoid losing my heels in the turf. Maja had helpfully left a bag of pegs in the basket and I began to peg the clothing on the line. A light late-evening breeze played with my hair and dress.

"Hello again, Joanne." My stomach swivelled over twice.

I turned to see a hand waving from the top of the fence at the back of the garden. It was Nick. Somehow he'd seen me hanging the washing out.

"Nice dress. Pink suits you. Are you working for Melissa? You didn't say."

This was a disaster. What should I do? I shouted out in my best girl's voice. "Sorry Nick, I have to put the washing out. Let's speak another time." Hopefully, that would put him off for a while.

He looked at me for a moment then scrambled over the top of the fence and dropped onto Melissa's side. He loped towards me.

"You can't come in here, it's Melissa's garden."

He smiled and continued walking towards me. The basket was still half full. I had to complete the hanging. I pulled out a tee-shirt and pegged it quickly but I wasn't going to finish hanging everything before he got to me. Would he see I'm a man not a wowoan when he got close up? I looked at the stepping stone path back to the house. I'd never make it in these six-inch heels in time. I carried on pegging up the clothing as he got closer and closer, his grin expanding with the reducing distance. I looked away.

He came up behind me and I felt his presence as I froze.

"Wow, great heels. How do you walk in them?"

"With difficulty." My voice croaked.

I finished the last of the clothing and turned, my head low hoping I didn't have a six o'clock shadow. I pushed past him. "Sorry Nick, I have lots of work to do."

"Fancy popping out for a drink sometime, Joanne? Maybe not in that dress, although I do love it. And your legs."

How was I going to get rid of him? I had to lie and then stay out of his way. "Yes maybe. I'll think about it."

Maja's face was pressed against the back window. A leering grin on her face. I guessed she'd somehow set this humiliation up.

I staggered back to the back door, lucky not to fall as I balanced on my new six-inch heels.

Nick remained by the rotary line. "I'll call round, when are you free next, pretty lady?" He shouted out as I entered the house, passing Maja's triumphant face.

I turned back to face him. "I'm not sure, I'm very busy at the moment." I spun back around and disappeared inside.

"OK see you soon, pretty lady," I heard him say. Then a moment's silence. What was that bell sound I heard when you walked?"

I hoped I wouldn't have to go out to the garden again. That way I'd be able to avoid him. I was sure he wouldn't come to the house to ask for me.

I closed the back door and looked at the floor. Tears stung my eyes and it wasn't the onions frying in the kitchen where Maja was preparing the evening meal. The very fact that he hadn't recognised me as a man hurt. Maja's continuing gloating presence made the situation worse and I wanted to slap her gleeful face. Had it come to this? Was I now so feminised that I was mistaken for a girl? A pretty lady? On the plus side, I looked good as a girl so I should get away with this until I can return to being a real man again. I had to think of the positives. There weren't many.

I went into the kitchen where Maja now stood legs apart and arms folded. She was waiting for something; I wasn't sure what she wanted. Her eyebrows lifted as if that would telepathically pass her message to me. The dress was irritating me as the petticoats under the skirt rustled in time with the bell. As I moved I had a rustling, heels clacking on the floor and the cat's bell ringing. The events of the past few minutes with Nick had made my near-permanent erection go down. That was some relief, although a constant tingle in my balls reminded me of my desperation to cum.

Maja mimicked a small curtsey. So that was what she wanted. I complied to avoid her complaining to Imogen or Melissa. My feet were unsteady on the heels.

Over the noise of the extractor fan and sizzling onions, I heard voices from the dining room. Melissa, Imogen and Mandy were waiting. Maja pointed at a tray with three tall glasses of lemonade on it.

"Put ice in glasses and slice of lemon. Then take to ladies. You are waitress tonight. And every night."

I tottered over to the side and sliced the lemons and retrieved the ice cubes from the fridge. It was so difficult to do anything in those heels, not only for the balance but the pain in my legs and feet. I walked carefully and with precision into the dining area carrying the round metal tray of drinks. The ladies were waiting, alerted by the rustle, the clip of my heels and the tinkle of the bell. I met silence and three pairs of unblinking eyes as I laid the glasses in front of each woman and curtsied before returning to the kitchen

I served the courses cooked by Maja, back and forth during the evening. I was no longer permitted to eat in the dining room, even on the floor from a dog's bowl. Now I had to eat in the kitchen after I had served their food and cleared up. I ate my salad on the floor with a dog's bowl at Maja's feet as she perched on a stool at the kitchen breakfast bar. My maid's dress fanned out on the floor around me in a circle of pink and white petticoated material. My food was lettuce leaves with cherry tomatoes and small slices of chicken. I was being allowed low-fat meat. Melissa had added a new rule that I had to use my fingers so now I was even denied the use of cutlery.

The next two weeks passed in a blur of sissy training. Every day started with a shower, my genitals were washed by Maja while I held my arms in the air. Then I had to put on a maid's dress to clean the house under the watchful eye of Maja. She no longer did the cleaning, she supervised me doing it.

Late morning was beauty treatment and beauty training by Mandy. She thinned my eyebrows and taught me how to apply my makeup. She taught me how to do my hair although she said she would continue to style and colour it herself. My fingernails had grown to about a quarter of an inch and Mandy used a shellac to colour them bright pink.

Mandy continued with the electrolysis on my body and after finishing my genital area, she did my chest and worked down my legs. It was a relief not to have to shave or be waxed but there was a nagging worry about when the hair would eventually grow back. My requests to Mandy for more information on this were met with, "Why would a pretty sissy girl want hairy legs and pussy?" *Pussy?*

I spent the afternoons with Imogen who taught me how to walk, sit and speak like a girl. In the past couple of days, I'd learnt how to walk passably in the six-inch heels. Imogen had incorporated hips wiggle and backside movement into my walk. It didn't feel natural yet but I knew what was needed. She added arm movements and a limp wrist style.

I noticed that my thigh muscles no longer ached so much in high heels. Instead, when I went for my humiliating bath and shower bare-footed, my thighs hurt from not being in the stretched position. It was worse on flat feet. Imogen told me with a straight face that my leg muscles had contracted and I had to wear high heels all the time. She had to be joking, I thought. She made me walk to the bathroom on tip-toes and it felt much more comfortable.

"My muscles will stretch again once I go back to flat shoes won't they, Ma'am," I said to her.

Imogen snorted as if it were an irrelevant question. "Sissy girls prefer high heels so why would you want to wear flat shoes?"

It was the only answer I got.

After training, I had a one-hour break to read female magazines in my room. After this, I changed into a maid's dress and served dinner to Melissa, Mandy and Imogen if they were there. I ate salad and lean meat from the dog's bowl at Maja's feet in the kitchen. The same routine every day. I hadn't seen Nick for a while so I was pleased that danger seemed to have gone away. I avoided the end of the garden as if it were a militarised war zone.

The diet was working and Imogen measured my waist every day. I was down to 26 inches and permanently hungry. Imogen wasn't happy with my progress, she wanted more and considered it was going too slowly.

It was at this time that Imogen introduced a corset to my daily wear. At first, I found it difficult to breathe. I quickly became used to it even though it restricted my physical movement. Imogen pulled it tight to a 22-inch waist every morning. With a fitted dress on, my figure was feminine. Melissa ordered me to go up to a D-cup with breast forms and, with the long hair and ultra-slim waist, I looked like a caricature of Dolly Parton.

I got into the routine of my new sissy lifestyle; I enjoyed the feel of the fine dresses and stockings. I never lost sight of the end game despite this. Get through the six-week period and then return to a male normal life. Surely there would be no more humiliating surprises in store.

14 A Date With Destiny

I lay across my bed, a magazine about makeup by my hand. My stomach rumbled and complained after four weeks of a near-starvation diet. I craved steak, fried potatoes, apple pie and ice cream.

Someone, I guessed Imogen, had stuck photos of naked young men on my bedroom wall. Where ever I look, there was an enormous cock facing me. Many had erections.

The corset dug into my ribs and the chastity cage rubbed my penis. I found a position that was more or less relaxing. The pleats from my white chiffon dress hung over my smooth thin legs. They were looking sexy and had changed shape. My legs were thinner but my smaller calf muscles were sharper and more defined. The high-heeled training with Imogen was having an effect.

Thin straps on my dress held up my now enormous chest. I hoped they wouldn't snap although the breast forms were probably lighter than real boobs. Annoyingly, my six-inch heels were still strapped to my feet. I was not allowed to remove them until I put on the little baby-doll nightie. It was still only 9.30 pm and too early to sleep.

Melissa let me have more free time lately although all there was to do was read women's magazines and soppy romance books. I longed for something deeper. Girls read good books too, even I knew that, but Melissa said she only wanted my little mind filled with ideas about pretty clothing and make-up.

Melissa was pleased with my progress and even I had to admit that being a girl was becoming more natural. I could do my makeup and my hair thanks to Amanda's teaching. I worried I was spending too much time thinking about making myself look pretty. Melissa and Imogen liked it so I guessed it was not a problem. I wanted to look good, even if it was a feminine look. You still had to take pride in your appearance, I'd learned that as a man.

I thought about a situation a couple of nights ago. It's been a month since I'd last cum so I asked Melissa if I could be permitted a 'release'. Before all this feminisation nonsense, I'd cum several times a week with Julie and with other girls I picked up. Melissa laughed at said although I'd made great progress, she would allow me to cum until she was happy that I'd become a good sissy girl.

I don't know what more she wants, it wasn't as if I was even pretending now. I've accepted what I'm forced to wear. Of course, I'd prefer to wear male clothing but it wasn't so bad being a girl any longer. What more could Melissa want?

The chime of the doorbell disturbed my thinking. It rang and continued for several seconds. I heard someone's shoes crickety-clacking at the front door. Muffled voices came up from below. Someone came in and the front door shut with a clunk. The voices continued in the hall. Whoever had visited had been let in and I heard some laughter.

"Joanne, come down." Melissa's voice carried up to my doorless room. I sat up, the smell of perfume and bubble bath wafted around the air behind me. I smelled and felt good but I was worried about who had arrived and would see me dressed up as a girl.

I looked at myself in the full-length mirror by the door. I would be attracted to me as a girl. I'd lost weight and the corset gave me a defined waist. I turned side-on and my long thick hair hung halfway down my back. I didn't have much of a bottom though. Or much in the way of hips either. Otherwise, I looked good.

I trotted carefully to the landing, my light dress flowed around my legs. I let my bare smooth arms hang loose by my side. I swung my hips as Imogen taught me for hours on end. I wondered why Melissa had wanted me to meet her visitor. It was important to look as feminine as possible, I didn't want to embarrass myself. Who could it be?

I descended the stairs slowly. I walked better in my six-inch high heels but I still had to be careful. I craned my neck over the bannister but Melissa and her guest had gone into the living room. I made my way down the stairs and to the entrance hall. I stopped for a moment and breathed in. This was to be my first public viewing as the new Joanne. I was nervous as I didn't know who it might be. I guessed it was one of her friends and she wanted to show me off.

This was a new beginning of sorts. Melissa had feminised me at her office but that was little more than making me wear female clothing and humiliating me. Now she had employed Imogen and Mandy to turn me into a girl and that had been successful, at least in my appearance.

I ambled towards the living room door, the voices were muffled behind it. The guest had a deeper voice than Melissa so maybe it was Nina from the office I guessed Melissa would want to show my big changes off to her. I didn't think it was Jane from the office as her voice was higher. It probably wouldn't be her niece, or at least I hoped not. She had deceived me after I thought she was helping me. She was only helping Melissa to make me more feminine. I heard the deep voice again. It had to be Nina.

I got to the door and touched the handle. I had nervous pangs from inside my chest. I couldn't believe what I was thinking but I did want to make a good impression. Yes, it had to be Nina. She was an imposing lady, tall with a deep voice; an Amazonian. I wondered whether Melissa had told her what she was doing to me, would it be a surprise to see how much I'd changed. To see how feminine I'd become since she last saw me.

I turned the round brass handle. It was a replica of Victorian door furniture; too perfect and shiny to be original. Melissa wouldn't have wanted anything old, everything had to be perfect. I swung the door open, it squealed on its hinges. I closed my eyes in a sudden feeling of concern and strode in with a fake confidence. My legs were like jelly.

I told myself to remember Imogen's training. Swing my hips, wiggle my bum and pout my lips. The talking in the room stopped. Only the sound of my heels clicking on the floor as I took small dainty footsteps. As Imogen had taught me.

I opened my eyes and scanned the room for Nina. Melissa stood on her own.

"What a beautiful girl, even sexier than I remembered you."

I swung round to the source of the comment, staggering on my heels. Nick stood there.

I couldn't breathe. I'd just come in in my exaggerated feminine way for the benefit of showing my progress to Nina and it was Nick.

Melissa spoke. "Nick came to ask if you were free. He wants to know if you'd like to go for a drink with him?" Melissa's face was beaming and mischief danced in her eyes. "I told him I was certain you'd love to. You being such as pretty girl and him such an attractive man."

I struggled for breath and croaked. "Er, er, It's a bit late I think I need to have an early night. Thank..."

Melissa cut me off with a raised hand. "It's no problem, Joanne. You can have a lay-in tomorrow. As I said, I told Nick you'd love to go out with him tonight. I said you've been talking about him asking who that lovely man was next door and how attractive he is. Well, here he is. Have a nice time and Nick..."

"Yes, Melissa."

"Don't do anything I wouldn't do."

Nick laughed. "Thanks, Melissa, it's good to have that much freedom with your pretty new housemaid."

Pretty housemaid? This was a nightmare. Melissa took me by the arm and pulled me to the front door and showed me outside. I was swept along with Nick following. I stood on the front step with him looking back at Melissa as she smiled like a predator. She shut the door.

I looked back at Nick who I saw was trying to gauge my feelings. The mid-August moon was full so the night was light. I was thankful I'd just wet-shaved as I didn't want to give the game away. I'd also applied foundation and makeup and looked good. I hadn't put on the false eyelashes but I'd applied heavy black mascara. I might get away with it.

The evening breeze played with my light mid-thigh dress and it waved around my legs and up to my caged penis. My eyes shot down to see a faint outline of the cage as the breeze blew the dress onto my body. I swallowed hard and patted it down.

"Let's take a walk to the pub, it's only 5 minutes away. I don't think you'd be able to walk too far in those heels."

I gulped. This was not only a date with a man but a walk in a public place dressed and made up as a girl. Worse still, his eyes kept dropping to my 40D boobs. My false boobs.

He took my hand with a, "May I?" and led me down the path to the road. I raised my eyes to the night sky in desperation. What could I do? What if he tried to kiss me, or worse put his hand on my false boobs or up my dress? Bile came to my throat and the fear I might vomit stayed for a few moments. Nick didn't notice my distress and chatted amicably about the nice weather and how much he liked the pub we were going to.

We entered the pub after the excruciating walk due to my heels and the situation. A pop song I recognised but couldn't place was playing too loudly. The pub was full of people – male, female, young and old. Good, I thought, no one will notice me. I was wrong. As Nick and I made our way to the bar, a group of men leered at my boobs and slim legs through their watery beery eyes. I shivered and looked on the bright side: I was fooling them so far.

I wondered if this is what a woman had to put up with; men ogling their bodies. It made me think about when I leered at young women and how they had felt. At that moment, I saw what Melissa was doing.

Nick got our drinks, two glasses of red wine. He led me to a small round wooden table in a corner. It was odd to be led by a man as I was used to doing the leading. After we sat, he said, "I want to know more about you, Joanne." His hand slipped to my knee under the table.

I pushed him off and giggled falsely. Thankfully, he didn't do it again. "Nothing interesting to tell," I answered, I work for Melissa and that's it."

He spoke about his job and interests. He asked me about what I enjoyed but I shrugged. I could hardly say I used to like drinking too much and screwing young women.

After we'd drained our glasses, I feigned sleepiness. "I have to get home."

He didn't object and I assumed he was getting fed up with my taciturn manner.

We left and ambled back in muted silence. He didn't take my hand this time and I suspected he was fed up with my lack of interest. We approached Melissa's front door and stood together on the step. It had got a little chilly and I shivered. Nick put one arm against the door frame and leant into me. "I enjoyed the evening, Joanne. You're very quiet but I like that in a girl."

A girl? Gulp. My mouth was dry, he'd been utterly fooled. He thought I was a girl and he'd taken my lack of interest as enigmatic. Melissa and her team had done a great job on me.

He moved his arm away from the door frame and wrapped it around my shoulder. He moved in closer and I smelled musky aftershave. He closed his eyes and he pursed his lips. He moved to kiss me. I stifled a squeal and leaned back. I pushed his arm off like I was brushing away a cobweb. I rang the doorbell, several times. Desperation.

He only grinned. "You're a shy one. No kiss on the first date? Not to worry, I can wait."

Despite his words, he looked affronted.

The door opened and Maja peered out. I pushed the door open wide and shoved past her. I stomped past her no longer bothering with a feminine walk.

"Night, Joanne," Nick called out forlornly.

A sudden guilt shot through me. He'd been charming and an almost perfect gentleman. I would have tried much harder than just putting my hand on a woman's knee and a little kiss on the first date. I shouldn't be horrible to him, I just had to let him down gently.

"Thanks for a nice evening, Nick, bye."

A smile came back into his eyes. I gulped, as I realised it had been too much. I'd given him a way back.

Maja watched us then looked at Nick. "She like you very much. She want you come back, see her again." She shut the door.

15 Mother-in-Law in Town

Julie sighed as she stared out of the window. Dark clouds covered the daytime sun and a shower threatened. The air was heavy. She worried about Joseph. She knew it was silly, she'd asked Melissa to correct his behaviour but wondered if things hadn't got out of hand. He'd been living at Melissa's place for the past six weeks and she'd heard nothing from him or Melissa regarding his training. Melissa told her it would, 'put him backwards' in his re-programming.

Reprogramming? That didn't sound so good. It was about showing him the error of his ways not changing him into something else. Had she gone too far in handing him over to Melissa to deal with? It had seemed a good idea to allow Melissa to give him a female perspective so he was able to see how his macho behaviour was so hurtful. She hadn't expected Melissa to go into it so enthusiastically. The warning signs were there knowing Melissa's hobby as a female dominatrix and the friends she mixed with. In retrospect, the Prince Albert ring through his penis was a step too far. Melissa had steamrollered her into it. It had seemed amusing at the time though.

The house was quiet without Joseph and that's what made her call her mother. This had been a big mistake. She discussed her marital problems with her mother over the phone, leaving out the bit about feminising Joseph. She told her mum they were living apart for a few weeks. Her mother drove up to stay the next day and provide 'moral support.'

Her mother, Verity, had always dominated her and her father. Verity said she would stay with her to help out while Joseph was in 'therapy'. Julie didn't how to describe what Joseph was going through at the hands of Melissa so therapy seemed a good word. Therapy for his drinking and behavioural problems.

The moment her mother breezed in, she said without any greeting, "I'm not surprised it's come to this. I've never liked him." She brushed through, dumping her case by the door and going to the living room and taking Julie's chair.

Julie followed her mother in with a sense of dread. Verity was going to be a problem.

"Why is Joseph staying at Melissa's during his therapy?"

That was not easy to answer. "We thought it might be useful to have a break, mum," said Julie. "We thought he needed some space to take in the changes and Melissa offered to help."

Verity did not look convinced with by answer. Julie made coffee and tried to divert the conversation to something else. It didn't take long for Verity to come back to the topic.

"It seems strange to me he'd stay at Melissa's." She looked confused. "Those two never got on."

Julie sighed. Her mother wasn't going to stop digging, like a bird searching for worms. Julie was getting a headache from the constant probing. Julie knew Melissa and her mum got on well and she had Melissa's contact details. It was only a matter of time before she became bored with Julie's prevarications and called Melissa. Melissa was not a shrinking violet either and would, in all probability, blurt out exactly what she was doing to her husband. She didn't want that.

Like a bloodhound on a trail, her mother continued asking questions in different ways. After a while she let it rest although Julie knew it was a temporary break until she resumed questioning. Verity got up and decided to tidy the place to her standards. She went to the kitchen. A few minutes later, the noise of crashing plates made her grimace.

She wasn't tidying but reorganising everything to how she thought it should be. Julie could never get her mother to listen, she steamrollered everyone and everything especially her.

The noise stopped and Verity appeared in the living area carrying a tray with a china teapot and two cups with saucers. When she saw Julie make her tea by squeezing a teabag in a mug she had found the tea pot she'd bought as a Christmas present and they'd never used and stored at the back of the cupboards.

Julie's mother placed the tray on the coffee table and sat next to her on the sofa. Verity's slim-fitting white dress had a thin red pattern stretched over her thighs revealing smooth bare tanned knees. She had succumbed to some cellulite but not so much as most 60-plus women. Her dark hair was too evenly dark brown for someone of her age. It sat over her shoulders with a flick up at the ends. She was domineering but stylish.

Julie thanked her mum for the tea, she guessed she needed a drink but was now thinking of something white and alcoholic. Julie felt her mother's eyes boring into her. She'd not spoken for several minutes so a monologue was long overdue.

"I know you're concerned for that loser of yours." Straight for the jugular with that comment, just as Julie expected. "Why don't we go and visit him? It might help you to see how his therapy is working."

Julie choked on her tea and spluttered. Verity smacked her on the back. "I don't think that's such a good idea," Julie croaked between her mother's back slaps. She knew Melissa will have kept him in female skirts and dresses as part of his re-education. She was not about to let her mother see that.

"Nonsense."

Julie closed her eyes knowing an onslaught of mother rationale was about to hit her. "I'll give Melissa a call and tell her we're coming to visit. Tomorrow, what do you think, dear?"

Julie sucked in air. "No, mum. Please. No."

Verity wasn't listening and, as Julie protested, she leant forward to where her mobile phone was sitting on the coffee table. Julie made a grab for it but Verity swatted her away. "I don't know what's up with you, Julie. I'm only calling Mel."

"No, Mum, please don't."

It was too late as the ring tone broke on one ring and she heard Melissa's voice answer. Verity backed away from Julie, holding her off with her free hand.

"Melissa, it's Verity how are you darling? And how is that loser of a son-in-law doing?"

It was too late. Julie backed down, defeated again. Melissa's voice drifted out from her mother's phone. "After six weeks of training, things are much better. Why don't you come and visit and see for yourself."

Julie gasped in despair.

"Yes, we'd love to come, Mel," Verity said. "It would be lovely to see if the loser has improved." There was a gap as Melissa said something Julie couldn't pick up. "That would be lovely, Mel," Verity said in reply. "See you tomorrow, darling," Melissa said something else. "Saturday lunch.?" Verity said. "Perfect." She hung up, triumphant.

Julie's slumped in the sofa.

Verity looked a little confused. "Melissa said she had some kind of grand unveiling to show us so my timing was good. I wonder what she wants to show us."

Julie guessed what Melissa wanted to unveil. She did not know how to explain what she expected to see tomorrow. She had a nasty feeling that this grand unveiling was a to be very different Joseph to the one she had left with Melissa six weeks ago.

16 The Female Touch

I was aware of someone standing over me as I woke. I'd been at Melissa's home and worn the cock cage to bed for six weeks but the ring around my balls still rubbed at times. On the plus side, my legs no longer ached. They had adapted to the extremely high heels I was made to wear every moment of the waking day. I now walked to the bathroom on tiptoes otherwise they ached again. My muscles had shortened although Melissa told me not to be concerned as this wouldn't be a problem in the future. Whatever that meant.

The curtains were flung open and a shaft of bright light glared into my face like a punch to my sleepy brain. I screwed my eyes tight to avoid the glare. I heard the double windows being pushed open and the early morning chirping of birds filled the room. A faint murmur of traffic drifted in from the high street. The smell of grass, trees and flowers drifted in and I relaxed.

My pleasure ended abruptly. "Wake up, sleepy girl, you have a big day ahead of you." Imogen stomped around my bedroom in her black boots. The dull thud of her leather soles against the floorboards throbbed in my head with each step.

She threw the bedsheets back, exposing my short pink baby-doll nightie rolled up to my chest. My pink plastic cock cage held in an incipient erection that was doomed to fail. Imogen's long shadow blocked the light from the window. I swung myself around to sit on the edge of the bed. I tugged the baby-doll down as far as it would reach which was to the top of my pink clitty cage.

"We're having visitors for lunch and Melissa would like you looking extra pretty and extra feminine for our guests. It's to be a grand unveiling."

"Guests? Unveiling?" I woke immediately. "Who?" I asked sharply. It elicited a slap on my cheek.

"Who, Ma'am," she reminded me.

"Sorry, Ma'am. Who are our guests, Ma'am?"

"You'll find out at lunchtime. It will be a nice surprise for you."

I shrugged and looked at the girly clock on my side cabinet. 6 am. I tiptoed to the bathroom and Maja entered after me with a towel and a flannel over her arm. She had her white plastic apron on over her maid's dress and the latex medical gloves on. I needed to pee and sat on the toilet as Maja and Imogen waited with arms crossed. It was to be an early shower today.

Imogen unlocked my cock cage and I went into the shower and washed my face and body, except my genital area. Maja performed her cleaning ritual with the usual grimace on her face while Imogen looked on with a face of stone. Maja cleaned my erect penis with cotton wool balls dipped in scented soap and threw them theatrically into the bin after.

"Mandy will do your hair later so don't wash it now, girl," ordered Imogen. "She's also going to work on your face. We don't like you shaving like a man as you're a girl now so she has some emergency treatment."

I shook as if a chill had passed through me at the casualness of her comment about me being a girl now.

I didn't understand what she meant by not shaving my face. How else would I remove my whiskers?

We returned to my bedroom accompanied by the tinkling sound of my reattached cat's bell to the ring on my engorged penis. The light pink flowery curtains were blowing out into the room like billowing sails. A chill hit my damp naked body. A pink printed tea dress was laid out on my bed. It had wide frilly shoulder straps and a tight small waist. A mix of diet and the corset now reduced me to a smaller size. My waist was at 24 inches and my chest at 40DD with the breast forms. I picked up the dress. It was light cotton and thin, almost see-through. After Imogen fitted me into my corset again, she pulled extra hard on the ties.

I couldn't breathe. "Ma'am, please could you let a bit of slack out? Please?" I puffed.

"Not today, girl, we're going for 22 inches in the waist. It's been six weeks and we have a target to meet. The pretty dress I've chosen for you won't fit if you don't use the corset pulled in to a 22-inch waist." She tugged harder with her knee against my back.

I'd always been slim; I'd liked the wasted rock-star look. Somehow they were looking to go from my previous 32 inches and take me to 22. I'd thought this too much in six weeks but they had almost got me there. I wasn't about to make a fuss as we were at the end of my six-week programme. This was to be the event that signalled my return to Julie and from this nightmare: a nightmare of feminisation and humiliation. I bit on my tongue as my hopes rose in proportion to the discomfort of the corset.

Imogen held a tape measure around my waist after she had tied up the corset and nodded. "22 inches." She had achieved it at the cost of my having bodily flexibility or being able to breathe smoothly.

I pulled the tea dress over my head and forced it down over my filled bra. The pink background of the dress was patterned with small blue and white flowers. A frill ran over my chest and a matching frill ran around my small waistline. The chest area laced up with two thin ties which I put into a bow. The light dress moved around my smooth thigh tops like gossamer silk which gave me a thrill. The dress was short but would have just about covered my penis if I was flaccid. I wasn't soft in the slightest so it poked out and Imogen was studying it. She had a hand to her chin and a fixed expression on her face.

"Your clitty is spoiling the fall of your dress." She continued to peruse my throbbing erection. The dress felt wonderful but I wasn't about to admit that. I was guessing Imogen had a hint from the effect it was having. Nonetheless, I wasn't going to give her the pleasure of knowing she'd beaten me and I had grown accustomed to the feeling of a dress. When I returned to masculinity, I would miss the feel of the dresses and the skirts they had put me in. They gave me a freedom I had never known before. But needs must and I wasn't going to wear dresses by choice when this was over.

"Maja?" Imogen called out and Maja's head bobbed back around the door frame. "Have you still got your rubber gloves on?"

Maja nodded and came back into the room, still dressed in her white plastic nurse's apron and medical gloves.

"Can you do something with this Maja please?" Imogen flicked my penis.

"Of course." Maja grabbed my erection with a gloved hand and put a small metallic bowl under the end of it. She began to rub my engorged penis with a gloved hand.

"Don't let her enjoy it, but we need this thing down," said Imogen with a frustrated look on her face.

Being masturbated by rubber gloves wouldn't have been my first choice but it was better than nothing. I yearned for the soft warm skin of her hands against my tender and sensitive penis. After several weeks without cumming, my desperation took whatever it could and after several rough strokes from Maja's hand, my face went hot and I groaned in anticipation.

Maja stopped rubbing instantly. I squealed as I wanted the orgasm. Instead, my cum drizzled into the bowl. She'd deliberately spoiled my orgasm and I remained desperate for the feeling.

Maja wiped away the residual discharge from my penis with a tissue and let my dress fell over it. I was covered and frustrated.

After breakfast, Imogen ordered me to go to the parlour where a chirpy Mandy greeted me. She was more excitable than usual. "I'm so looking forward to giving you a super-pretty hairstyle," she said. But, first I need to do your whiskers. I'm going to do electrolysis on your face."

I shuddered. "It's not permanent. I will be able to grow a beard in the future?"

She waved my objections away again. "This will save time and be smoother than shaving your face twice a day."

I guessed that was best. I settled into the chair and let her do her stuff. The procedure took two hours and from what I could work out, she put the electrolysis gun into my hair follicle and then tugged the root out with tweezers.

The root? "Miss Amanda, isn't removing the root permanent?"

"Shush, Joanne. Sit still. I'm concentrating."

After she'd finished the electrolysis on my face, she washed and styled my hair. She put a tighter wave into it with curling tongs. The mirror behind the sink showed my hair flowing sexily down over my false breasts in long curls.

Next, she applied false eyelashes, smoky-eye makeup and bright red lipstick. It looked like a wound slashed across my face. Mandy unclipped my small pierced earrings and replaced them with giant hoop earrings and hung a matching girly necklace with flower patterns around my neck. It hung partway down my bare smooth chest.

She was finished. I stood unsteadily on my enormous heels, the thin strap was tight around the tops of both ankles. Mandy sprayed copious amounts of a sweet perfume on my chest, neck and cheeks and then around the air above my huge hair. I was breathing with shallow breaths due to the tight corset.

Mandy led me to a full-length mirror and stood beside me with a grin as wide as a river. I couldn't believe what I saw. The touches she provided today were the final element. I was looking at a woman.

I was attracted to myself. There was nothing to suggest I was a man underneath. I looked fantastic.

"I think we've got you there, Joanne."

I nodded in agreement for a moment with a slight smile of satisfaction then stopped myself. What was I doing agreeing to her comment? And who was coming for lunch?

Melissa walked into the beauty parlour and looked me up and down. "Twirl for me, Joanne."

I had to twist back and forth on my toes so she could admire the results. My dress whirled in the air. Her face broke into a wide grin and she gave me my instructions for lunch. Don't forget to curtsey to our guests and call them both Madam. I would have to serve lunch and drinks. So her guests were women, that was some consolation. I didn't want a repeat of the Nick saga.

17 The Grand Reveal

I couldn't believe what they had done to me. Standing in my bedroom, staring at the full-length mirror, all I could see was an attractive girl. I was still a man underneath, biologically, but no one would realise that by looking at me now. Nick certainly hadn't realised.

I rubbed my chin. It took me back to the days when I was a young boy, it was so smooth. There were no whiskers or any sensation of whiskers. My face had been red from the electrolysis so Mandy had applied soothing cream and foundation.

The cracking sound of an approaching thunderstorm shook the windows. I hoped for some relief from the humidity as the sky darkened and the first drops of rain hit the path outside. I watched from my window as the storm approached and grew.

The guests would be arriving any minute and my body shook at the prospect. Melissa had told me that if I passed as a girl then it meant that she considered that I had reached an important milestone on time and to plan. What was I? A project plan?

I pondered on the prospect that my ordeal was finishing. I would return to my old life and, I had to admit, I'd learned a lesson amongst all this humiliation. I'd learned how women think and what they do and feel. The episode with the amorous Nick also helped in that regard. I was on the other side of the fence for a time. I discovered that female clothing was nice. More than that, it felt sensual and erotic. I would return to male clothes without a doubt. I wasn't so sure I wouldn't be going through Julie's wardrobe when she was out to try a few things. I'd miss the female clothing.

Outside it was now darkening with the storm and the street lights came on. This was growing into a major electrical storm. My eyes caught a car pulling into the driveway, its headlights lit the driveway and illuminated the raindrops like falling jewels

The car was the same model and colour as Julie's car but I didn't catch the registration plate. My stomach wobbled for a moment but if it was Julie, then that wouldn't be so bad. She'd got used to me wearing female clothing as my punishment and the guest being her was the least bad outcome. But Melissa said guests. My stomach twisted again.

The car doors slammed shut and I saw two ladies running to the house with their coats over their heads. One of them was Julie, but who was the other one? The coats hid them from view from my vantage point.

The doorbell rang and my throat closed. Julie hadn't seen me looking this feminine and I didn't like the idea of her seeing me this way. She was going to have to accept me back as her husband and I worried that she would continue to see me as Joanne. I heard the front door open and Melissa and Julie greet each other. They were two best friends yet so different. Julie was meek and timid, Melissa was the alpha assertive businesswoman.

I couldn't make out the other voice from my room. Who could it be? I hoped it was not Julie's mother. The witch. How she'd like to see me this way. I imagined her reaction and comments. She'd revel in my humiliation. No, Julie wouldn't do that to me. Julie wasn't strong, that's how I'd got away with so much before this. Even so, she wouldn't subject me to Verity, her mother knowing I'd probably be looking like this. Surely not. My throat tightened as the rain gushed down in a torrential downpour. I closed the window.

I went to my mirror and peered at my reflection. My big hair was long, wavy and flowing over my shoulders. I was beautiful for a woman although more than a little slutty. Too much hair, massive boobs and a short skimpy dress.

I blinked my false eyelashes and they fluttered like two bats hanging from my eyelids below pencil-thin eyebrows. The red scar of lipstick slashed across my otherwise smooth white hairless face. Two round large earrings hung through my enormous hair. I had a 40DD false bust bursting out of the low frilly front of my white tea dress. I was thankful it wasn't as short as other dresses I'd had to wear and therefore covered my chastity cage. The only trouble was that the material of the dress was so thin and fine it hung tight against my legs, behind and cage like a floating cobweb. I needed to be careful. I stepped back, my heels clapping against the floorboards.

"Joanne, you can come down now." Melissa sounded excited to be showing off her work on me to Julie and whoever else was there. I was to be the catwalk show.

I walked down the stairs and into the dining room, I remembered Imogen's instructions. Small steps. I walked even more gingerly than normal as I was trying to avoid the bell attached to my cage tinkling. A murmur of excited chatter came from the room and as I entered it died away and three pairs of eyes fell on me. Melissa, Julie and...oh no. Verity. I froze.

"Joanne girly, what do you have to do?"

Melissa's voice brought me out of my trance. I curtsied, finding it difficult on the high heels. I cringed at hearing the bell tinkle. Julie's mouth dropped like a ventriloquist's dummy with its jaw strings cut. She was stupefied.

"Would you ladies like a drink." Melissa's face assumed a supercilious expression.

Julie shook her head as if she was shaking some sense into of she saw. Me as a girl.

I glanced at Verity. She looked blank. She hadn't recognised me. Julie hadn't told her. This was going to be difficult. They asked for coffee and I curtsied and hobbled to the kitchen. As I left the room, I heard Verity asking Melissa when we'd see the new Joseph. She'd assumed I was one of Melissa's housekeepers, like Maja, and paid me little attention. That was lucky, but would it last? I returned with a tray of cups of coffee. I placed them by each lady and remembered to curtsey when finished.

"Joanne, why don't you stay and chat with us?" Melissa's mischievous grin lit up her face. She was enjoying this.

Julie hunkered over her coffee cup looking rapidly at me and then Melissa. Her eyes darted like arrows at each of us. Verity looked impatient and tutted at the idea of one of the hired helpers sitting with the ladies.

Melissa wasn't concerned. "Verity, Joanne is a very special girl and she's been with us for exactly six weeks now."

"The same time as Joseph," Verity replied. Not getting the hint.

"Exactly the same time, Verity, that's right. Is that a coincidence?" Melissa's eyes went to me and back to Verity as Julie looked like she wanted to find an enormous hole in the ground to sink into. I wanted to use the same hole.

Verity looked directly at me, still without recognition. Good, I might be able to get away with this, I thought.

"So what do you do here, Joanne?" Verity was convinced I was a servant and spoke to me condescendingly.

Melissa answered for me, to my relief. "I took her in as she'd been a very bad girl. I like to help out seemingly lost causes. We've taught her manners and how to be a real girl and we've made her look very pretty and feminine. Don't you think, Julie?"

Julie coughed, spurting her coffee back into the cup. Verity looked me up and down and a chill ran through me expecting Verity to get Melissa's hints.

"She's certainly a pretty one, Melissa." Verity looked away and was beginning to lose interest in me, a factor Melissa picked up.

"Yes she had been behaving very badly but it's never too late to change I say. And Joanne has certainly changed a lot recently." Melissa was giving more hints. Julie turned her face away and put her hand to her mouth, her face turned crimson.

"So when are we going to meet the new Joseph, Mel?" Verity still hadn't realised it was me despite Melissa's obvious hints.

Melissa's eyes narrowed. I fidgeted, feeling hot, facing the three ladies like a prisoner at a parole board awaiting a renewed sentence. Melissa didn't have to do this, she could just say I was busy elsewhere and stop this teasing and humiliation. Verity wasn't going to see it was me without being told directly. Melissa was having a lot of fun at my expense. I kept my head down to avoid even the outside possibility that Verity would recognise me as Joseph.

Melissa wanted to keep things going. "Joanne, tell Verity and Julie how much you've learned here. How you enjoy being a well-behaved girl."

Oh no. I breathed in hard. I had to remember all that Imogen had taught me. Speak in a high voice and be demure. I opened my mouth but nothing came out. Julie's eyes looked like they might pop out of her sockets. I cleared my throat. "I have learned a lot, thank you, Mistress Melissa."

Julie fell into a coughing fit again while Melissa looked proud. She wasn't finished. "Tell them how you're happy to be a well-behaved submissive pretty girl, Joanne."

I wanted to run, to escape, to get away from this excruciating nightmare. Melissa was leading me deeper into humiliation and enjoying every moment. Thankfully Verity still hadn't realised. Julie tried to change Melissa's line of questioning by asking about her job. Melissa grunted a response and was not going to be put off. "Joanne, as I just asked, tell Verity and Julie how much you like being a submissive pretty girl and serving women."

Verity looked confused, unsure why Melissa was humiliating her hired help in this way. I looked away and ruffled my dress over my smooth bare legs. Much of the male muscle tone had gone due to my diet of salad and lean meat. I gulped. I thought my head might explode with pressure at this torture.

"We're waiting, Joanne." Melissa wasn't going to let me off the hook. The hook that she had embedded in me and was now reeling in. I looked down at my hands on my dress across my thighs. I saw with horror that the pink cock cage showed through the thin white material of the dress and I pulled my hands away to avoid it stretching so tight.

"Yes, I like being a pretty submissive girl and serving women," I mumbled. I wanted this to be over and the whole six weeks over and to return to normality. It was a matter of time but Melissa was turning the screw for a big finale before that happened.

"Louder Joanne, I don't think they could hear you."

Julie touched Melissa's arm and her eyes locked with mine. Her eyes pleaded silently for help. "We heard fine Melissa, now tell me about your work."

"Louder, Joanne." Melissa had a determined look and her eyes now fell on mine.

"I like being a pretty submissive girl and to serve women," I said. The sooner I got this over with, the better.

"And do you want to remain a submissive sissy girl, Joanne?"

Julie sloped back in her chair, defeated. She didn't have an ounce of assertiveness in her. I had no choice.

"Yes, I want to remain as a submissive sissy girl." I sang it out loud. I had to say whatever she told me to get this over with and pass her test. I had shown Melissa I was a reformed character and I was beaten.

Verity was extremely confused now. A perplexed expression came over her face. She wasn't sure why Melissa was pushing this point. She was the only one in the room who didn't know it was me, Joseph.

"Excellent to hear this Joanne. You can therefore remain a sissy girl. But," she said, "there's still so much to do before you are truly where I want to be."

What was she on about now? Hadn't we finished the six-week punishment period? Wasn't I about to go home to live with Julie again? Hadn't she made me look and act like a girl? I'd surely passed her programme.

Verity stared hard at me. "There's something about you that's familiar, Joanne. Your voice. The face. Have we met somewhere before?"

I almost heard her mind clicking over. "I don't think so, Madam," I said too quickly and forgot my voice training in the enthusiasm to get her off that line of thinking.

Verity's face went through a series of expressions that matched her thought process. "No. It can't be."

The room went silent. Julie had sunk so far in her chair that I was worried she might fall off.

Verity got up and walked towards me. A mix of expensive perfume and hair spray got stronger as she got closer. Her face moved into my personal zone and we were nose to nose. I saw her foundation makeup was thick. Her perfectly shaped eyebrows raised high into her forehead. "No. It can't be." She spun around to look at Julie who had a hand over her eyes. She turned back and put her face to mine again. "Joseph?"

I didn't know what to say, this was possibly my worst ever moment, apart from that date with Nick.

Verity's shock fell away into a wide grin. "Nice work, Melissa. Very nice work indeed."

Julie peeked through her fingers.

"This is the best thing that could have happened to Joseph, that good-for-nothing husband of Julie's. A useless nobody. Well, well. So you like being a submissive girl? Who would have thought that? This is a turn up."

There was only one thing for it. I had to brazen it out. "Yes, it's me, Verity. But it's a punishment for my mistreatment of Julie. I don't want to be a sissy girl. I'll be returning to manhood now and I've learned my lesson."

Verity glanced from me to Melissa waiting to hear her response. Melissa crossed her legs. "But Joanne, you've just told us you tell us you want to remain a sissy girl."

A rock grew in my chest, a huge weight making it difficult to breathe. A girl? "No, no I was just saying that to keep the peace and go along with your game. I want to stop this and go back to being a man."

Melissa stood up and went next to a grinning Verity. "What do you think, Verity? Her behaviour is much improved but I believe there's still a lot of work to do."

Verity's face screwed into spite. "I agree, Mel."

"What more can I do, Mistress? I've done everything you asked. I'm a changed person." My desperate voice cracked.

Melissa looked at me but spoke to Verity. "Her bum's a bit flat and those tits are not real. And look at that silly chastity cage." She lifted my flimsy dress to display my pink chastity device and Verity snorted a high-pitched laugh. She stroked my Adam's apple as I shook in anger. "And she's not yet experienced a man."

A man? What did that mean?

"Yes," added Melissa, "there's so much more work still to do to Joanne. She's going to be under my control for a while longer yet. Until she becomes sissy Joanne for good."

END OF BOOK 2

I hope you enjoyed Becoming Joanne 2. I'd love it if you could leave me a review on the site where you bought this novel.

Why not sign up for my Forced feminisation and FLR newsletter?

Visit my blog at www.[1]ladyalexauk.com[2] to subscribe

I love to hear from my readers so, please email me if you have any comments on my books or FLRs and male feminisation: ladyalexa@mail.com

And remember, the only good man is a feminised sissy man.

---

1. http://www.ladyalexa.com/

2. http://www.ladyalexauk.com/

Don't miss out!

Visit the website below and you can sign up to receive emails whenever Lady Alexa publishes a new book. There's no charge and no obligation.

https://books2read.com/r/B-A-JTBM-EFFLC

BOOKS 2 READ

Connecting independent readers to independent writers.

Did you love *Becoming Joanne 2*? Then you should read *Becoming Joanne 1*[3] by Lady Alexa!

Julie enlists the help of her best friend, Melissa, to help her transform Joseph. Melissa's plan is to feminise him.

Melissa is a high-powered lawyer but also a professional Mistress. She decides the only way to teach Joseph a permanent lesson is to transform the aggressive Joseph into the submissive Joanne. This story charts Melissa's transformation of Joseph and how Joseph becomes Joanne. This 34,000-word novel contains scenes of a sexual nature including reluctant male-to-female gender transformation, female domination, humiliation and forced sissyfication. Strictly for adults of age 18 plus or the age of maturity in your region if higher.

Read more at https://www.ladyalexauk.com.

---

3. https://books2read.com/u/mdXvKd

4. https://books2read.com/u/mdXvKd

Also by Lady Alexa

Becoming Joanne
Becoming Joanne 1
Becoming Joanne 2
Becoming Joanne 3

Femboy Love
Femboy Love

Feminized and Pretty
Feminized and Pretty 1
Feminized and Pretty 2
Feminized and Pretty 3
Feminized and Pretty 4

Lockdown Feminization
Lockdown Feminization 3
Lockdown Feminization 1

Sissy femboy transgender husband
Sissy Husband 2
Sissy Husband 3
Sissy Husband 1
Sissy Husband 4

Sissy Princess
Sissy Princess 2
Sissy Princess 1

Stepmother's Sissy
Stepmother's Sissy
Stepmother's Sissy 2
Stepmother's Sissy 3

Standalone
Maid To Serve
A Very Dominant Woman
Feminized By My Wife
Female Transformation
Samantha's Law
An Accidental Girl
The Mother-In-Law Dilemma

About the Author

I am an author and blogger on female led relationships, encouraged feminization and femdom and other erotica.

Read more at https://www.ladyalexauk.com.